FATED MATE

CATAMOUNT LION SHIFTERS, BOOK 3

J.H. CROIX

J.H. CROIX

DEDICATION

You know who you are...you make me laugh and you helped make my dreams come true.

Sign up for my newsletter for information on new releases!
http://jhcroixauthor.com/subscribe/

Follow me!
jhcroix@jhcroix.com
https://amazon.com/author/jhcroix
https://www.bookbub.com/authors/j-h-croix
https://www.facebook.com/jhcroix
https://www.instagram.com/jhcroix/

ONCE UPON A TIME...

Centuries ago in the northern Appalachian Mountains, mountain lions fled deeper and deeper into the mountains, seeking safety from the rapid encroachment of humanity into their vast territory. Mountain lions developed the power to shift from human to mountain lion and back again, saving their species as they hid in plain sight. The majestic wild cats became creatures of myth. Reported sightings were treated as wildly speculative rumors. Impossible. Until one evening on a busy highway, a car struck an animal in the dark. The first confirmed sighting of a mountain lion in the East in close to seventy-five years. The wild cat was dead, its unbelievable existence snuffed out by a car. This mountain lion wasn't just any mountain lion. Though its autopsy would only reveal it was, in fact, a mountain lion and that the lion had improbably traveled over 1,500 miles from South Dakota, the longest known journey for such a creature. In Catamount, Maine, shifters lived amongst the world, having successfully protected their very existence for centuries. Until one of their own died an improbable death, and they learned of a threat facing their kind.

1

Liliana North watched the snow float down around her as she stood beside her car on the side of the road. It was an early winter morning in Catamount, Maine with snow barely falling as the clouds cleared. The sun was cresting the horizon, its rays bright against the wintery white landscape. The road wound through the outskirts of Catamount, a wooded tract of land on one side and a field on the other. The scent of balsam fir was sharp in the cold air. She leaned over to check her tire.

"Definitely flat," she said to herself. A crow squawked in reply. She glanced up to see the crow had landed on the roof of her car, watching her curiously. She glared at the crow who might be providing her some company, but would be of no help with her flat tire. She pulled her phone out of her pocket and sighed. Reception was notoriously spotty anywhere on the outskirts of Catamount. Catamount was situated in the foothills of the Appalachian Mountains, the hills and valleys making merry with cell phone reception.

Liliana, Lily to those who knew and loved her, tugged her jacket tighter around her and looked down the road. It was just past seven in the morning, and she didn't expect too many drivers at this hour. Shaking her head, she set to work changing her tire. Moments later, she managed to send two of the tire lug nuts rolling on the icy surface and had to shimmy under her car to recapture them. She was on the ground, the snow cold against her back when she heard a car come to a stop and footsteps slowly make their way toward her.

"Need any help?"

The voice was low, gravelly, most definitely male...and sexy. *Seriously? How can you think a voice is sexy when you don't even know the man attached to it?* Lily rolled her eyes and brushed her hair out of her face. She knew the answer to her mind's taunting question. She was twenty-eight years old and somehow, despite her best efforts, she was still a virgin. Lately, she had sex on the brain. Between a few members of her inner circle falling in love recently and her own annoyance with her virginity, she couldn't seem to stop herself from assessing, and occasionally lusting after, every man who crossed her path. *Yeah, but this is just some random guy who stopped to help you by the road.* She wished she had an off button for her tendency to converse with herself. She considered whether to tell the man with the sexy voice to carry on. She could use the help though because she wasn't so sure her spare tire was in good enough shape to use.

She stretched and curled her fingers around the last of the errant lug nuts. Holding them firmly in her grip, she wiggled her way out from under her car and almost choked when her eyes landed on Noah Jasper. Tall, dark, smoldering, enigmatic, and most definitely sexy as hell—that was Noah Jasper. Lily had many fantasies about Noah in high school. He'd been two years ahead of her and had half the girls in Catamount drooling over him. He stayed above the fray.

To Lily's knowledge, he'd never dated anyone in Catamount. He'd gone straight to college and then on to the Marines. Rumor had it he'd been in the Special Forces. A few months ago, she heard Noah had moved back to Catamount.

There she was flat on her back in the snow and a flush raced through her at the mere sight of Noah. He leaned forward, stretching his hand out. She placed her hand in his and shivered at the contrasting warmth. Her hand was engulfed in his. Without appearing to exert effort, he steadily pulled her to her feet. Once she was standing, she tucked the lug nuts in her pocket, glanced up into his amber eyes and tried to keep from blushing. His mouth quirked slightly.

"What?" she asked.

Noah gestured to her hair. "You've got pine needles sticking out of your hair."

She reached up and felt several sticking straight up. She brushed her hands through her hair. When she thought she had tugged the last pine needle out, she glanced back at Noah who stood quietly. She gave her jacket a shake to knock the loose snow off. Of all the people to see her with pine needles in her hair and snow covering her back, Noah was most definitely not her choice. He was a sexy and mysterious shifter who'd moved away, while she was a boring, quiet computer programmer. In the world they lived, she was the least likely to be noticed. Catamount, Maine was a town filled with mountain lion shifters. While Lily came from one of the oldest shifter families in town, she tended not to attract attention and preferred to keep it that way. Noah, on the other hand, attracted plenty though he didn't seem inclined to care.

She forced her attention to the moment. "Thanks for stopping. I got a flat tire, but I'm having trouble changing it, and I'm not so sure my spare's in good enough shape anyway."

Noah met her eyes again and nodded. Damn, he was handsome. He had chiseled features. As with most shifters, his face had a feline cast, his cheekbones angling up, eyes tilting at the corners. His almost black hair made his amber eyes stand out. His mouth was sensual and full. He nodded to her spare tire. "Mind if I take a look?"

Her heart pounded so loudly, she could

barely think. She nodded quickly. "Go ahead."

Noah rolled the tire away from where she'd leaned it by her car and ran his eyes over it, giving it a push. The rubber gave easily under the pressure of his hand. He looked up and shook his head. "It needs air." He lifted it and strode to the back of his truck, tucking it under the cap. Without a word, he quickly adjusted the jack and lowered her car.

"What are you doing?"

Noah swung her way, his amber eyes sending her belly into a tailspin of flutters. "Making sure your car's safe for now. We can't leave it jacked up like that. I'll drop you off wherever you need to go and stop by here later after I get your tire repaired."

"Oh, um, you don't need to do all that." Lily felt off-kilter and confused to have him so quickly step in to help.

Noah met her eyes again. She didn't know how she could handle riding in a car with him. His proximity had all but turned her to mush. Wet heat coiled through her when he arched a brow. "I'm not going to leave you here, and it's not safe for you to try to drive on that spare." He glanced at his phone. "Since there's no phone reception here, you can't think I'm going to drive off. What's your plan, wait for the next person to come along?" Suddenly, his eyes widened and then a look of bitterness followed. "Ah, I get it. You think I had something to do with the mess my uncle landed in?"

Lily shook her head forcefully. "No! I wasn't even thinking about that." As she spoke, she considered that if she hadn't been so bowled over by him, she probably would have wondered. The last few months in Catamount had been marked by turmoil and betrayal after the death of a shifter unraveled the secrets he left behind. Callen Peyton had died in mountain lion form when he was killed by a car in Connecticut, of all places. Lily's brother, Jake, was the one who uncovered Callen's plans to sell the services of Catamount shifters to a drug smuggling network out West. The ensuing events had involved a kidnapping and a cross-country trek to Montana.

Noah's uncle, Theo Jasper, had been arrested a few weeks ago for his involvement in the smuggling network. That was the public story. The full story circulated only among the mountain lion shifters in Catamount.

The glaring detail missing for everyone else was that Theo had shifted into mountain lion form and taken Lily's brother, Jake, and another friend on a wild chase through town first. This little event was yet another in a cascade of events in Catamount that had driven deep fissures in the shifter community in Catamount.

Catamount shifters had stayed safe for centuries by keeping their existence a well-guarded secret. Callen's death and the tentacles of the drug smuggling network threatened to blow that secrecy to pieces. Lily considered that Noah had a point. Though she hadn't been thinking of it right now, she figured he'd had many eyes cast in doubt on him since Theo was arrested. She was so twisted inside at being near him, her tendency toward suspicion had been turned off. She took a breath and met his eyes.

"I really wasn't thinking about that, Noah. I'm not so great at accepting help, that's all." Her words were true, but the other truth was it was hard to know who to trust in Catamount anymore. Even though Noah sent her body into a tizzy, her gut told her he was trustworthy. Her breath misted the air. The crow that had been sitting on her car earlier squawked from a nearby tree. Snow sparkled where the sun's rays landed.

"I'm guessing it's not so fun being you these days in Catamount," she finally said.

Noah shrugged, his eyes guarded. "Theo's an ass. I barely know him. He's my dad's brother, and I wasn't exactly close to my dad before he passed away. I get why people would wonder, but trust me, I had nothing to do with any of that bullshit. My mom's about half out of her mind about it, but I figure we have to wait until the dust settles." His words were matter-of-fact and polite. He met her eyes again. With the barest nod, he continued. "Did you want that ride after all?"

Lily nodded, hugging her arms around her waist, shivering when a gust of wind blew across the road, stirring snow in a swirl. "Let me get my purse." She rushed over to her car and grabbed her purse. Noah waited by his truck. When she reached his side, he opened the door for her. She hadn't realized how cold she'd gotten until he closed the door and the warmth of his truck cab seeped through her.

When he climbed inside, he sat still for a moment before turning to her. "If I came across like a jerk, I didn't mean to. This whole..." He paused and gestured vaguely. "...mess makes me sick."

"You didn't come across like a jerk. Everyone's on edge these days." She didn't add that he set her on edge in an entirely different way.

He held her eyes for a long moment, and she felt the flush crawling up her neck and face. He was way too sexy for her to think straight. Her traitorous body swirled with heat. Noah was seriously out of her league. There was a reason she was still a virgin, and it definitely wasn't because she was saving herself for anything. It was because she wasn't the kind of woman men noticed. Female shifters were supposed to be sexy, but even though she couldn't quite say what she was lacking, she knew Noah had only noticed her because her car was broken down.

He nodded slowly. "On edge is one way to put it." He turned away and put his truck in gear. "Where to?"

NOAH GLANCED over at Lily and took a breath. Lily North was about the cutest woman he'd ever laid eyes on, and he couldn't figure out how he'd never noticed her before. Her golden brown hair fell in loose waves around her shoulders. She'd tried to tidy her hair after she pulled the pine needles out, but had only slightly succeeded, which was just fine with him since it only made her even cuter. Her blue eyes darted sideways to meet his, and she bit her lip. He forced himself to take another breath. Damn. He'd known Lily for as long as he could remember, but only in passing. It wasn't that he didn't notice her, but he'd never gotten close enough to her to realize she was flat out gorgeous with her sky blue eyes, her flushed cheeks and her petite curvy body.

They were both from shifter families in Catamount. Difference was, Lily's family was revered in Catamount while his family, on the other hand, was probably better forgotten. Theo's involvement in the drug smuggling scandal was just another notch in their list of misdeeds. Noah's father, Willis Jasper, had died from a heart attack five years ago. Noah had felt only relief and regret at his death. Willis had been abusive to his mother for as long as Noah could remember. Just as with humans, there were plenty of shifters who wanted nothing more than easy power.

Knocking around anyone close was Willis's way of finding power. Noah had cultivated the skill to stay out of the way. The only thing he could thank his father for was his skill at staying quiet and almost invisible, which had served him well in the Marines and enabled him to climb his way into the Special Forces. Stealth missions came easily to him.

Noah moved back to Catamount a few months ago when he found out his mother's health was failing. She'd said nothing to him about it, but his aunt had called him and told him his mother had been diagnosed with lung cancer. Since he'd come home, he'd learned from her doctor that her cancer was Stage Three and had spread to her spine. Sadly, she'd never smoked in her life. The doctor had explained that she was likely exposed to radon gas for years. New England had high rates of radon present in the soil. Many homes dealt with this by installing systems to filter it out, but their home had never had one.

His mind flashed to this morning when he found her coughing up blood in the kitchen. He immediately shoved the memory away. She was sick and most likely dying. He had to find a way to come to terms with that.

In the narrow world of his childhood, his mother had been the only bright spot in his heart. Though she'd never managed to walk away from Willis, she'd done what she could to shield Noah and been a source of steady support and love for his entire life.

He hadn't thought twice about moving back to Catamount when he heard she was sick. While his career in the Marines had saved him in many ways, he'd been moved to administrative duties on base after sustaining multiple injuries in a bombing in Afghanistan. While he could have bided his time and been cleared for full duty again, he couldn't even consider leaving his mother to die alone. His father may have been a big part of the reason he left Catamount, but his mother was who kept his heart tethered there.

He'd also missed Catamount—the stark seasons, the weathered beauty of the forests here, the nooks and crannies hiding in the Appalachian Mountains, and being in the one and only place he felt safe being true to himself as a shifter. While he'd lived away for over a decade, he could count on one hand the number of times he'd shifted into mountain lion form while he was away. It wasn't safe, so he barred the door to that part of himself. It wasn't like shifters walked freely around as mountain lions in Catamount, but at least half the town were shifters, and the expansive wilderness nearby allowed shifters to roam freely when they wanted. In the few months he'd been home, he'd spent hours and hours roaming the forest and foothills—feeling and flexing into his mountain lion again.

Lily's phone jangled—a cherry chirp of a ring—and she jumped in her seat. Noah canted his eyes sideways to find her fumbling for her phone in her purse. As soon as she got it out, she dropped it. The phone slid out of sight under the seat. He bit back the urge to laugh. She looked so flustered and damn cute.

"Dammit!" She leaned forward, but quickly sat up again. "No way I can reach it. I can't even see it." She sighed and leaned back.

"I'll get it for you when we stop," he offered.

He looked over at her when he stopped at an intersection near downtown Catamount. She was looking out the window, chewing her lip and twirling a lock of silky hair around her finger.

"Where should I drop you off?"

She turned to him. When her gorgeous blue eyes collided with his, she flushed, uncertainty flashing in the depths of blue. She bit her lip, and a jolt of lust hit him. Noah didn't know what had come over him, but his body had all kinds of things to say about Lily. He couldn't remember the last time he'd even noticed a woman. He'd done his share of dating, but nothing ever went beyond light and easy. After the nightmare of watching the devastation his father wrought on his mother, he didn't believe in the fairy tale of love and romance. Hence, he threw himself into his career and kept relationships superficial. The effect Lily was having on him was—unusual. He wanted to know what lay behind those flickers of uncertainty. His body wanted to tug the bundle of her—lush curves and softness—into his lap and kiss her senseless.

He shackled his urges and focused on the moment. "You can drop me off at my brother's office," she finally said.

The light changed and he drove through the intersection, turning toward the center of downtown where Jake's office was. "You work with Jake?"

She shook her head. "Not really. Sometimes I help him with projects."

"I know Jake's does something with computers, but what do you do?"

"Jake does coding, website building and is what most people call a forensic computer expert. Short description: he can hack like nobody's business, but he keeps it legal. I work in the same field, but we do different things. I work the other side of hacking by identifying network vulnerabilities and helping create fixes. I freelance and mostly work from home. When Jake needs extra help on something, he usually calls me."

"Damn. Guess you could say being brilliant runs in the family, huh?"

Noah pulled up in front of Jake's office as he said this. He turned to Lily. Her cheeks were flushed again. She shrugged, still twirling that lock of hair around her finger. "Not really. We both like computers though." She glanced toward Jake's office and back to Noah. "So, um, do you want me to see if Jake can deal with the tire?"

Noah couldn't explain it, but there was no way he was giving up the chance to see her again. Even if seeing her only meant picking her up with the repaired tire and returning her to her car. "Nah. I got it. How long were you planning on being in town today?"

"I hadn't really planned much. What time were you thinking of heading back out?"

"I have a few errands to run, but I should be done this afternoon. How about I pick you up around two?" He left out that what he would be doing for most of the day was sitting with his mother while she received her latest round of chemotherapy.

Lily nodded. "Sure. That'll work." She moved to get out of the car. "Oh, I have to get my phone!"

She climbed out and looked under the seat. Noah watched her for a moment and leaned down to see if he could find her phone. Just as his hand closed over it, all the way over to the driver's side, he looked up to say something and found Lily's face inches from his.

Her blue eyes widened when he met her gaze. The flush simmering under the surface of her skin flared on her cheeks. Her lips, plump and an almost perfect bow shape, were so tempting, his breath hitched and pulse pounded. His eyes, clearly under their own control, flicked down. She wore a scoop neck shirt, which hung forward since she had leaned over. The generous curves of her breasts were on display, a glimpse of blue lace teased him. *Holy hell.* Her ivory skin was taut. He could see the beat of her pulse in her neck.

She froze and suddenly scrambled away. His body literally ached for a split second. He'd come so close to touching her, the loss of the chance was a sharp pang. He forced himself to take a breath before he sat up. He held his palm out, her phone on it. "Here you go. So, uh, I'll see you this afternoon?"

Lily brushed her hair back, tucking those honeyed locks behind her ears, and pulled her jacket together in front, hiding her delectable breasts from his view. He doubted she had a clue the effect she had on him. It was like a lightning bolt out of nowhere. He was beyond relieved he was sitting down with his jacket covering the bulge in his pants. She nodded quickly and snagged her purse. She turned to leave when he realized she hadn't taken her phone from him.

"Hey, did you want your phone?"

She whirled back. "Oh! Yes, yes, of

course." She reached out, her fingers brushing his when she took the phone. "See you in a little bit. Thanks for the ride." She turned away quickly and all but ran up the walkway to her brother's office.

2

"Who dropped you off?" Jake asked the moment Lily stepped inside his office.

She tugged her coat off and hung it on the hooks by the door. "Noah Jasper." She turned and met her brother's eyes. He arched a brow, skepticism marked on his features.

"What's he doing giving you a ride?"

Lily walked to the corner to the small table that held a coffee pot and mugs. She eyed the empty coffee pot and sighed. "I got a flat tire on the way in, and he stopped to help. I was going to put my spare on, but the spare didn't have enough air. When Noah stopped, he offered to give me a ride and get the tire repaired. He'll take me back to my car this afternoon."

She knew the situation would annoy Jake. He would have wanted her to call him. He was a rather typical overprotective older brother. His tendencies in that direction had been exacerbated with recent events in Catamount. Lily only chafed a little under Jake's overbearing nature, but it could get frustrating at times. When Noah had stopped to drop her off, she'd felt like she had to offer to have Jake help because she didn't want to impose on Noah. But when he'd insisted, she'd been a tiny bit thrilled. For once, somebody other than Jake could watch out for her.

Lately, Jake had been distracted. For one, he was at the center of the events unfolding since Callen's death. He'd been the one to stumble upon Callen's multiple email aliases and discovered Callen's communications with the drug smuggling network. He was also best friends with Dane Ashworth. Dane's fiancée, Chloe Silver, had been kidnapped by another shifter from out of town and Callen's younger brother, Randall Peyton. Thinking about all of it made Lily tired, and she knew Jake was close to running on empty. He'd also finally seen the light of day and admitted he was in love with Phoebe Devine, a good friend of both of theirs for many years. Lily couldn't be happier for them.

She met Jake's blue gaze. He leaned back in his chair. "Be careful. We don't know if Noah had any involvement with his uncle."

"I'm not an idiot, Jake. I know we don't know who to trust. Noah was nice enough to stop and check when he saw my car. The phone reception sucks out there, so if he hadn't stopped, I'd have been stuck waiting for the next person to drive by. I'm not saying I know for sure he's safe, but I think he is. Theo was his dad's brother, and you know how things were with his dad."

Lily may not have been close to Noah growing up, but Catamount wasn't too big, and the shifter circles in Catamount were even smaller. Noah's father was known as an abusive asshole around town. She remembered seeing Willis Jasper slap Noah's mother, Carol, once when she stopped at a gas station. Everyone knew he beat his wife, but no one seemed to know if Noah faced his wrath as well. What was known was Noah hadn't been close to his father and had moved away as soon as he could. He rarely visited until after his father passed away. Lily believed Noah didn't have anything to do with whatever his uncle had been doing. It didn't fit. The look in his amber eyes when hurt and bitterness flashed through them came to mind. Just as Noah had wondered if she was avoiding him because of Theo, Jake was questioning him for precisely that reason.

She sat down across from Jake. He was watching her. She sensed he wasn't sure how to respond to her supportive comment about Noah. She wasn't one to argue much. She kept her head down and went about her business. For whatever reason, she felt inclined to push the point with Jake. She held his gaze. "I know we can't go around assuming everyone's innocent, especially with what's happened the last few months, but maybe you don't have to assume everyone's out to get me either. My gut tells me Noah's not involved."

Jake was silent for a long moment before he shrugged. "Fair enough. He's under the microscope already. If there's something to be worried about, we'll know soon enough."

They moved on from the topic, diving into Jake's latest project. He needed her help to lock down a security network for a new corporate client. Lily dove into her work. She loved computers. Coding was straightforward for her. It also suited her personality. She'd been born an introvert in a family of extroverts. Jake was the quintessential North family shifter—bold, assertive, and everyone's friend. She was the opposite. Social situations totally stressed her out. She felt awkward and out of sorts. She had a small circle of good friends, but beyond that, she kept to herself. She didn't talk about it with anyone, but she felt conflicted about being a shifter. To her family, it was everything. To her, sometimes it felt like a burden. She couldn't imagine not being a shifter, but recent events had only increased the sense of burden. Romantic relationships were her nemesis—at least, in her head. She'd never mastered the art of flirting and the mere idea of a casual relationship confused her. Not because she had some kind of prudish problem with casual sex, but because she was too damn shy to let down her guard to get to know someone superficially. Hence her virginity, her personal millstone.

Noah's amber eyes flickered in her mind as she paused to check on something in the code she was examining. That moment in his truck when she was searching for her phone and glanced up, his gaze had burned into her. For a blink, she thought he was going to kiss her. Sheer want had rushed through her. Then, she got flustered and moved away. Little did he know, he left her with her pulse pounding and wet heat building inside. But there was no way Noah found her attractive, what with pine needles in her hair. She shook her head sharply and focused back on her work. She loved computers because they were ruled by logic and easy to understand. There was no confusion about intent, or misunderstanding.

After a solid few hours of work, she glanced over at her brother. Jake was deep into whatever he was working on. She pushed away from the table where she was working and stretched. "I'm gonna go grab some coffee at Roxanne's. Want some?"

Jake finally looked up. "Absolutely!" He fumbled in his pocket. "Here." He handed a crumpled twenty-dollar bill to her. "Would you mind picking up some lunch for me too? Just tell Roxanne to make whatever sandwich she wants for me."

Lily chuckled and nodded. "Be back in a

bit."

When she strode outside, the winter wind hit her right in the face. She tugged her hood up and leaned into the wind. Jake's office was in the center of downtown Catamount. Catamount was a quintessential New England town. It had a picturesque town green with granite walkways decoratively crisscrossing the area and ancient oaks and maples towering above. Most of the homes were several centuries old and well-maintained with small signs indicating the year they were built and the original owners. In some cases, the descendants still resided in the homes, as was the case with her family, along with many of the shifter families.

Catamount had been founded centuries ago by mountain lion shifters. A small nameless settlement was given an ancient nickname for mountain lions. Those who weren't privy to the existence of shifters thought the name quaint and sensible, seeing as Catamount was situated in the vein of forest through which the northern Appalachian Mountains traveled. Mountain lions once flourished in the wild here, so no one questioned the town's namesake. Little did they know roughly half the population was comprised of shifters who descended from clans of mountain lions who developed the ability to shift out of desperation to save their kind.

Catamount had grown from a small New England village to a mid-size bustling town. Lily savored the icy air. Though it chilled her, she loved winter and its stark reminder of nature's power. The bare branches were dark against the sky. Snow spun in swirls from the gusts of wind. She carefully stepped through a snow bank when she crossed the street. Roxanne's Country Store was in an old colonial style home. Its bright blue door beckoned in the gray light of winter. She pushed her hood back and stomped her feet to knock the snow off before making her way to the coffee shop and deli in the back.

The deli held a soft hum. Lily strode to the counter and read the list of specials scribbled on the chalkboard above while she waited. Roxanne came through the door to the back and smiled widely. "Lily! Don't usually see you here for lunch. How's it going?" Roxanne's blonde hair was tied loosely in a ponytail that swung when she turned to check the oven timer. Her blue eyes were bright when she stepped to the edge of the counter.

Lily shrugged. "I came to town today to help Jake with some work. I figured I'd rather come see you and get some amazing coffee instead of making whatever instant stuff he has on hand."

"What'll it be then?"

"Straight coffee for me. I'm getting some for Jake too, so whatever you think he wants. He also wants a sandwich and said to tell you to make what you want. I'll take one too."

"Hang on, let me start a fresh pot."

Roxanne quickly turned away to get the coffee started. Lily glanced around the scattered tables and saw Noah in a corner table. He was flipping through the newspaper, one hand curled around a mug of coffee. As she watched him, she jumped when she heard Roxanne's voice.

"That Noah, he's easy on the eyes, huh?" Roxanne asked with a soft chuckle.

Lily whirled around. Roxanne stood by the counter, her blue eyes glinted with mirth. Lily shrugged, tamping down the skip of her pulse at seeing him. "Maybe so. He gave me a ride today when I got a flat tire. Jake's all suspicious, but I don't think Noah had anything to do with whatever his uncle was up to."

Roxanne's expression sobered as she slid

a cup of coffee across the counter to Lily. "No surprise you're wondering, along with everyone else. I seriously doubt Noah has anything to do with it. Not because I know for certain, but because it's just not like him. I've gotten to know him these last few months since he moved back to town. He stops by here almost every day. He's a good man."

Curiosity piqued, Lily arched a brow. "What makes you say that?"

Roxanne turned away to check the oven, quickly turning some loaves of bread in the massive brick oven. When Roxanne turned back, she glanced to Noah before replying. "He came home to take care of his mother. She was diagnosed with lung cancer last year. She kept a lid on it, but Noah told me her sister finally called him. I'm not so sure she's going to make it, but Noah's been helping her with everything. His father died a few years back, so without Noah, she'd be on her own. Noah's straight as an arrow. Can't imagine him getting involved with drug smuggling."

Lily glanced from Roxanne to Noah. Her heart clenched to consider what his mother was going through and what it said about him that he'd come home to take care of her. The teeny tiny corner of her heart that she tended to shush was "awwww" about Noah now. She forced her eyes away from Noah and back to Roxanne. "I'm tired of wondering about everyone."

"You and me both. But Noah's not one to wonder about," Roxanne replied firmly.

Another customer came to the counter, so Lily stepped to the side. She glanced at Roxanne. "I'll wait for a bit. Just let me know when the sandwiches are ready."

Roxanne nodded and turned to the next customer. Lily glanced in Noah's direction again. Between his kindness to her this morning and learning how he was helping his mother, her attraction to him notched higher. She gathered her courage and walked over to Noah. She reached his table and paused beside it. He didn't appear to have heard her approach. Her social nerves were running high.

"Noah?"

His head whipped up, his eyes landing on her. It was so subtle, she couldn't know for certain, but she thought there was a slight flush to his skin. He held her gaze for a moment, completely silent, before speaking.

"Hey there. Didn't know you'd be stopping here for lunch. Have a seat," he said, gesturing to the chair across from him.

She slipped into the chair, wrapping her hands around her cup of coffee, its heat anchoring her. "I didn't know I'd be stopping here for lunch either. Jake has terrible coffee at his office, so I thought we'd be better off if I came here."

Noah's mouth hooked up at the corner. His dark hair was on the longish side. Lily recalled the last time she'd seen him, he had the requisite military buzz cut. His black curls only amped up his sexy factor. His amber eyes watched her steadily. Her pulse skittered wild. He idly traced the edge of his coffee cup, and she was transfixed by his hands. She had to force herself not to stare. She was a sucker for a man's hands. Not that she'd ever had the chance to rule someone out before, but hands could be a deal breaker for her. Noah's were strong and masculine with a worn edge to them—more than acceptable, sexy even. A faded scar ran in a jagged path across the back of his hand.

"How's your morning been?" Noah asked.

"Busy. I've been working straight out

since you dropped me off. Whenever you're ready to drive back works for me."

Noah glanced at his watch and back to her. "I have one more appointment and then I'll pick your tire up. I dropped it off this morning at my friend's shop." For a moment, she thought he was going to say something else, but he didn't. A brief flicker of sadness flashed in his eyes. She couldn't help but wonder what appointment he needed to attend. With what Roxanne had told her about his mother having cancer, she wondered how he was doing.

"Okay. As soon as Roxanne has our sandwiches ready, I'm headed back to Jake's office. You can pick me up there whenever you're ready."

Noah started to say something, but his eyes looked beyond her shoulder. He held a finger up, but didn't say a word. Lily turned in her chair and followed his gaze. Two men were sitting in the corner. Both were shifters, Derek Miller and Kirk Hogan. Lily knew them only in passing. Though they were quiet, the tension between them was clear. Kirk was leaning forward, his finger pointing at Derek's face. Derek lounged in his chair. Lily knew his relaxed posture was not what it seemed. Just like the wild cats from which they descended, shifters had crazy quick reflexes. Derek's expression was hard. Lily glanced Noah's way. His eyes were trained on Derek and Kirk.

In a flash, Kirk flipped the table toward Derek. Noah moved so quickly and quietly, she hardly noticed how he made it across the room. Derek leapt up from his chair. Just as Kirk hauled off to punch Derek, Noah caught his forearm in midair, freezing it in place. He barely appeared to be exerting effort.

"Stay out of this!" Kirk practically spit his words out.

Noah simply shook his head, maintaining his iron grip on Kirk's arm. Derek glanced to Noah, his brows hitching up, but he remained silent. Kirk altered his stance and struggled against Noah before giving up and allowing his arm to drop. Noah released him slowly, his eyes locked on Kirk. Lily glanced around the deli. All eyes were watching the scene. The quiet among the men was disconcerting.

Derek took a step forward, nodding to Noah. "Thanks, man."

Kirk sneered at Derek. "Fuck you." He snatched his jacket off the back of his chair and stormed out. His shoulder caught the corner of a display in one of the aisles, knocking a card stand over and leaving a scattered mess in his wake. He didn't bother to stop. Lily glanced around the room before hurrying over to pick up the cards.

Roxanne's voice carried across the store. "Drama's over for now. Let's all mind our own business again."

As Lily knelt and shuffled the cards up into her hands, attempting to organize them again, Roxanne came over to help. "You don't need to do that, Lily. I got it."

Lily met Roxanne's eyes. "I don't mind. You've got enough work to do. What the hell do you think that was about?" She kept her voice low.

Conversation had picked up with the murmur of voices giving them cover to talk. Lily knew speculation was running rampant in the room. With everything that had gone on lately in Catamount, the argument just witnessed could have been as mundane as a disagreement over a bill, but everyone would assume it had something to do with the drug smuggling scandal Callen had dumped in the town's lap.

Roxanne shrugged. "My best guess is

Kirk is in the middle of the whole damn mess. He's usually up to no good. He and Derek used to be buddies, but things have gone sour lately. I'm relieved Noah was here. He's not one to make a fuss, but he's not gonna stand by and let shit go down. I was afraid one of them was gonna shift. Maybe not on purpose, but because they were pissed off. Thank God that didn't happen. I don't even know how we'd clean up that rumor."

Roxanne was a good friend, and she didn't gossip much though she probably knew just about everything about everyone in town. She was a shifter herself from another of the founding shifter families in Catamount. Her grandfather had named the store after her when she was but a baby. Since the store served as one of the central shopping and gathering locations in town, more gossip passed through here than probably anywhere else. Lily had learned over the years that Roxanne's disarming manner led people to tell her all kinds of things. She only commented on what she knew when it was relevant.

Lily tidied the stack of envelopes she'd gathered and started returning them to the card rack. "What do you mean about Kirk being up to no good?"

Roxanne glanced over her shoulder before turning back and handing Lily another pile of cards. "He likes to party and he doesn't like to work. He and Derek were in high school together, a few years ahead of us. You know how Derek's family runs the old quarry outside of town?" At Lily's nod, Roxanne continued. "Well, he offered Kirk a job a few years back. He ended up having to fire him. Kirk wants a quick buck, but he doesn't want to have to work for it. Granite work is hard work. It's fair to say that pretty much put the nail in the coffin on their friendship. They used to come in here all the time to have lunch when they were working together. Today's the first time I've seen them together in years. My bad feeling radar is tingling pretty strong."

With Roxanne handing over cards, Lily put the rack back in order and stood up, dusting her jeans off. Noah was standing by Derek talking quietly with him. When she glanced his way, his eyes immediately met hers. With a quick nod to Derek, Noah walked across the room, his amber eyes locked on her. Her pulse kicked up and flutters swirled in her belly. She took a breath, a pointless attempt to settle her nerves. *You are being ridiculous. Act normal.* Problem was, Noah had the worst effect on her. He was way too sexy for her sanity and not the kind of guy that would ever notice her. His casual attention, due solely to him being nice enough to stop when she needed help, was making her body go wild.

He came to a stop at her side. Roxanne immediately spoke. "Thank God you were here! I don't know what the hell Kirk was gonna do, but it went from a possible mess to nothing. You're such a badass." Roxanne chuckled when she patted him on the arm. She looked to Lily. "You know Noah was in the Special Forces in the Marines, right?"

Lily nodded, but couldn't seem to think of what to say. Of course, Noah just had to be tall, dark, handsome, sexy as hell, and a military shifter badass. Precisely the kind of man she could never even consider having. Seeing as she usually flew under every man's radar, why did her body go haywire over a man who could have any woman he wanted? She tried to talk her pulse down, but it was having none of that and kept galloping away. She felt a flush creeping up her neck.

Roxanne had turned away to reply to a customer. When she turned back, she looked at Noah, her eyes sobering. "Any idea what that was about?"

Noah shrugged. "Not too sure. Derek isn't offering many details, but he said Kirk's pissed off because he won't offer access to the quarry."

"Why would he need that?" Lily asked.

Noah shrugged. "Exactly what I asked Derek. If he knows, he's not ready to talk about it."

Roxanne rolled her eyes. "Well, he's not too helpful." She paused and glanced at the counter where a customer waited. "I've gotta go. Your sandwiches and Jake's coffee are waiting if you're ready." She hurried off.

Lily looked up at Noah, willing her skin not to blush again. She'd blushed more in one day around him than she had in years. "I guess I'll see you when you're done with your appointment."

He looked at his watch. "Damn, I'm about to be late. Catch you later." He turned quickly and weaved his way through the aisles to the door. Lily picked up the sandwiches and coffee and headed back to Jake's office.

3

A few hours later, Lily leaned back in her chair and stretched. Jake's eyes were glued to his computer screen. He'd abandoned what he'd been working on earlier to dig into Kirk Hogan. After she'd filled him in on the almost-altercation at Roxanne's and told him what Roxanne had shared about Kirk, he was in detective mode again. When she stood and started cleaning up his lunch debris, he looked up.

"Well, looks like Kirk might be another link in the chain. I can't dig up anything about why he'd want access to Derek's quarry, but just like Callen, he's got several email aliases. I've been trying to keep up with it, but it's tedious work tracking every loose end. Looks like they were both in contact with one of the guys out in Montana. I'm gonna put a call in to our contact out there and see what he can tell me."

Lily's chest tightened. She wanted to see an end in sight. The ripple effects of Callen's nefarious activities kept washing up on the shores of Catamount. She hated feeling suspicious about everyone and didn't like the fear coiled inside of her. It wasn't discussed much in Catamount because in recent decades shifters had largely succeeded in becoming invisible, but in earlier centuries, shifters had been hunted and killed at points. Myth worked in their favor because it was difficult for humans to believe shifters lived among them. The lure of mountain lions and their secret existence in the East served a convenient purpose for shifters. If they were ever seen deep in the woods in mountain lion form, it offered a great tale to whoever saw them. Even though Eastern mountain lions had been declared extinct, many people clung to the belief that they were still surviving by stealth. In a way, that was entirely true. It's just that most people didn't assume the stealth involved mountain lions who shifted into human form and back again at will.

The underbelly of the shifter world had been laid bare when it was discovered Callen had been trying to sell their services for smuggling. Who better to smuggle drugs than a mountain lion? They moved quickly and quietly and were avoided at all costs, even in areas where they were common out West. The fear running in circles through Catamount was that Callen had exposed Catamount to the wrong shifters and now they had to root out whoever else was involved. With a sigh, Lily looked to Jake.

"I suppose this is good news then? Maybe another lead to chase down that might get you somewhere?"

Jake nodded and started to speak when there was a quick knock. He glanced up, his eyes questioning.

Lily stepped to the door to find Noah waiting. His amber gaze landed on her and sent her pulse running wild again. Her belly clenched, and her breath became shallow. After a long moment, she realized she was staring. "You didn't need to knock," she said, forcing the words out, trying to get control of her body again.

Noah shrugged. "I wasn't sure. Are you ready?"

She nodded and stepped back from the door. "Just let me get my boots and coat on."

Noah hesitated at the door.

"Come on in, Noah," Jake called out.

Noah kicked the snow off his boots and stepped inside Jake's small office. He closed the door and leaned against it. His eyes were slightly guarded, which grated on her. Perhaps Noah didn't need her to defend him, but she felt strangely protective of him. She didn't like knowing he had to worry shifters were lumping him in with his uncle.

Jake swiveled in his chair to face Noah. He appeared to be considering his words. "Lily tells me you were a big help over at Roxanne's today."

Noah shrugged. "All I did was step in. No sense in letting a fight get started."

Jake nodded slowly and picked up a pen, twirling it in his fingers. "Well, I'm sure Roxanne appreciates it."

Again, Noah shrugged.

Jake arched a brow. "Thanks for helping Lily today."

"No problem. Her spare tire has enough

air now, and the flat one's repaired. I'll put the regular one back on when I drop her off."

Lily pulled her jacket on and laced her boots up. "Okay, I'm ready." She looked to Jake. "If you need more help, I should have some time next week. I'm tied up the next few days on a project."

Jake nodded. "Thanks for helping out today. Phoebe said for you to give her a call. She wants to do a girls' dinner."

"I'll call her later." She dropped a kiss on Jake's cheek and strode to the door. Noah stepped aside and held the door open. When she brushed by him, she could feel the heat of his body. It sent a current buzzing through her veins. In a flash, she was flustered... again. *Seriously? You've turned into a complete flake today. Noah was just standing there, and you're all gaga.* She willed her body to calm down, but thinking about it only seemed to make it worse. By the time she was sitting in Noah's truck, her nerves were a mess. *See, this is why you're still a virgin. You're such a social wreck that there's no way you'll get past a kiss with anyone. If it's someone like Noah, who's so smokin' hot that you're about to go up in flames, you probably will literally melt into a useless puddle.*

Lily held her hands in front of the air blowing out of the heater vents, trying to warm her cold hands. The temperature felt like it had barely budged today. The thermometer outside her kitchen window had registered zero this morning. If the temperature had made it up to ten degrees, she'd be amazed.

Noah climbed in the truck and without a word he started driving. The silence amped up her tension. Her pulse bounded ahead, as she tried to calm her nerves. *He's driving you to your car. That's all this is. Why are you such a mess? Sure, he's hot, but whatever. Deep breath and get your head on straight.*

Noah's voice interrupted her internal conversation. "Does everyone call you Lily?"

"I haven't thought about it much, but I guess it's mostly family and friends."

Noah's only response was a nod.

Lily considered what to say next and her words ended up surprising her. "Roxanne told me about your mother being sick. I'm sorry to hear that. I hope she's doing okay."

He stopped at a light and glanced her way, his eyes somber. "Thanks. I met her for one of her chemo appointments today." He took a breath before looking away when the light changed. "My mom's the stoic type, so she acts like she's going to be fine, but she's pretty sick. That's why I moved back home."

Lily considered what he must be going through. Though she only knew broad strokes of his life, a man didn't move home to take care of his ailing mother unless she meant a lot to him. Her heart clenched. "I bet she really appreciates that you're here. I'm sure it's difficult to watch what's she's going through."

He was quiet for another long moment before he replied. "She means a lot to me. There was no way I'd not have come home."

A deer darted across the road in front of them. Noah braked abruptly, reaching his arm across to steady her when she lurched forward with the jolt of the vehicle. His touch was warm and sent sparks whirling through her. It was as if she'd swallowed a butterfly, her belly tumbling with flutters. She leaned back immediately, trying to get her body's response to him under control. His arm fell away.

The deer paused at the side of the road, its lithe form elegant. The doe lifted her head and sniffed the air before stepping carefully into the trees. After a few cautious steps, it leapt forward and disappeared into the snowy forest. Lily tried to get her mind off of Noah, but the space in his truck felt tiny. An electric charge hummed through her body. He kept driving and moments later, he pulled to the side of the road where her car sat waiting. When he turned to her, his eyes held a glimmer of heat. Or that's what she thought. *As if. Get a clue. You're imagining things because your body's gone wild. There is NO WAY Noah's got the hots for you.*

She took a breath, willing her body to calm down. She stared at the dashboard and waited.

"Lily?" Noah's voice struck sparks on the tinder of her desire, low, taut, and warm at once. Her pulse, already wild, ricocheted off the charts.

She dared to look his way and found his eyes on her, as if he'd been waiting. A hot shiver raced through her. His eyes caressed her before he angled toward her. Her heart beat so hard she thought he surely had to hear it. He cleared his throat, his amber eyes never breaking away. "I hope you don't mind..." His words trailed off as he leaned forward and tucked a lock of hair behind her ear. Her skin tingled where he touched her.

She was frozen, her entire body pulsing in want. Hot, liquid need swept through her. She shifted her legs restlessly, trying to control the wet heat in her center. The subtle motion only made it worse.

In the taut moment, she thought his eyes held a question. Her own must have offered the answer because he moved decisively, sliding his hand into her hair, cupping the back of her head and bringing his mouth to hers. The simmering heat inside of her burst into a conflagration at the feel of his lips against hers. She hadn't had much experience with kissing, in fact if she pondered it, she had to struggle to recall the last time she'd been kissed. But this kiss from Noah—it was unlike any kiss she'd ever experienced. He kissed her as if he had all the time in the world, as if her mouth was the center of the universe. What started as a soft exploration, turned into a heated explosion when she gasped and his tongue swept inside.

Lily tumbled into sensation. The kiss went on and on. She forgot where they were, forgot her tired and worn mental anxieties about men, and scrambled to get closer. The desire that had hummed to life early this cold winter morning twisted into a flame inside. The hand cupping the back of her head, sifted through her hair and trailed down her neck, his lips following. Shivers chased in the wake of his touch, her skin pebbling. Her breath was ragged, she couldn't think past anything but the feel of his hand sliding down around her breast, lingering over the curve. Somehow she was on her knees in the tiny space, shoving her hands up under his shirt, gasping at the feel of his rock hard muscles under her hands.

Noah pulled back, his eyes hot embers on her. If a gaze could have burned her, his would. He traced her lips with his thumb. Never breaking eye contact, his thumb coasted down her neck, pausing over the beat of her pulse before following along the edge of her shirt, which dipped down in a scoop, the tops of her breasts exposed. The heat of his electric gaze on her, he hooked his thumb over the edge of fabric and tugged it down. The cotton gave easily and suddenly her breasts were exposed. One of the luxuries she allowed herself was lingerie. She couldn't say why she loved lingerie so, but she did and damn if she cared that she was usually the only one who could appreciate it. She wore a barely there lacy blue bra today.

Her nipples were taut and peeked through the lace.

Noah's ragged groan sent a thrill through her. His eyes dropped from hers. She glanced down to watch his hands cup her breasts. He thumbed her nipples through the lace, and it was her turn to groan. Her breasts were tight and achy. Watching him touch her drove her wild. Slick heat built between her legs, need pulsing through her. She moved restlessly, desperate for more. Thought had abandoned her, so she found herself climbing into his lap, straddling him in the tight confines of the space. He pinched her nipples and gave a soft tug before he closed his lips over one, the wet suction of his mouth driving her mad. The heat of his shaft rested against her. She slid back and forth, almost crying out at the delicious spikes of pleasure.

After drenching the lace of her bra, he flicked his thumb at the tiny clasp. Her breasts tumbled free. She gasped at the feel of his mouth on her with nothing between her skin and his wet touch. He gave the same painstaking attention to her nipples that he'd given to her lips—kissing, licking, sucking and stroking—until she was almost incoherent. He pulled away, though away could only be measured in inches, and paused. His heart beat under her hand, his breath was as ragged as hers. When she met his eyes, they held a look that bordered on pain.

Need thrummed through her, beating along with the drum of her heart. His amber eyes held hers. His shoulders rose and fell with a deep breath. "I think we might need to slow down," he choked out.

His words broke through the fog in her brain. As glimmers of coherent thought began to return, she realized she was straddling him, her hips rolling restlessly against his rock hard cock. Her breasts were exposed, her nipples glistening from his attention. She'd become someone she didn't recognize—wanton and almost desperate. She flushed from head to toe and knew her face must be flaming.

"Oh..." The only word she could manage to form. *You sound like an idiot. Well, you definitely just acted like one. You're on the side of the road and all but threw yourself at him.* As if on cue, a car sped past them. Fortunately, the windows were fogged.

Lily took a breath and started to wiggle away. Noah's hands clamped on her hips, his grip firm. "Don't."

She forced herself to look at him though it took all of her will, mortified she'd lost control and was half naked. "I'm sure you didn't mean for that to happen. I was..."

He shook his head sharply. "What are you talking about?"

She wasn't sure she could blush harder, but she must have because she was on fire, but this time it had nothing to do with desire, only utter embarrassment. "You said we needed to slow down..."

"That's all I meant. If you think I didn't want to kiss you, think again. If we don't slow down, I won't be able to stop at all."

Perhaps his words should have brought her to pause, but all she wanted to do was *not* stop. As if to emphasize his point, he arched his hips against hers, sending a jolt of pleasure through her when the pressure of his cock nudged her clit. Two layers of clothing between them—his and hers—and she was so close to the edge, she could probably orgasm right here in seconds if he kept doing that. Sensibly, he didn't.

He cleared his throat. "I know I've known you since we were kids, but I don't really know you. I don't want you to think I'm some jerk out for nothing more than a piece of ass.

I'd like a chance to get to know you." He cleared his throat. "If I'm being honest, about all I could think about today is what it would feel like to touch you." His words were gruff, his eyes held a glimmer of uncertainty, but he didn't look away.

Her heart pounded, she could hardly believe his words. She didn't move as she tried to absorb what he said. She looked away and tried to gather herself. When she looked back at him, his eyes had become guarded.

He shrugged. "I can take a hint." He started to lift her off of him.

"No! I wasn't trying to give you a hint. I was trying to figure out what to say." Barely able to get enough air, she spoke through her nerves, her words tumbling out rapidly. "I don't have a lot of experience with this kind of thing. I don't mean to come across like an idiot, but I'm nervous. I guess I couldn't believe you liked me like that, but I'd love it if we could..." She paused and shrugged. "I don't know, get to know each other."

His grip on her hips eased slightly, and the guarded look left his eyes. The air was charged as he held her eyes in his hot, amber gaze. He took a breath as if to steady himself. His eyes flicked down to her breasts—in that flicker, it felt as if he touched her. When he looked up again, he smiled, almost regretfully. "How about I get that tire changed before I forget I'm trying to be a halfway decent guy?"

A giggle escaped her as she nodded. "Right. Good idea." She promptly discovered that untangling herself from him in the tiny space with her breasts bare and desire hardly in check proved to be a challenge, physically and emotionally. By the time, she'd gotten herself off of him, her breath was shallow and her pulse out of control. When she glanced over at him, he looked on the edge of pain.

"Are you okay?" Her question was more automatic than anything, a reflex in response to the look on his face.

He slanted his eyes to her and chuckled. "You don't seem to be aware of what you're doing to me." His words were rough and raw.

Hearing any man talk about her like that was so foreign to her, Lily had no idea how to respond. The fact that it was Noah—sexy, reserved Noah who she now knew to have a kind enough heart to take care of his sick mother—well that made it nearly impossible for her to do anything other than blush madly.

Noah shook his head as he adjusted his shirt. "Anyone ever mention you're sexy as hell when you blush?"

On cue, her face got even hotter. She managed to shake her head. He merely chuckled at her response before climbing out of the truck.

4

———————

Noah watched Lily wave as she drove away. Lily. Her name suited her. He checked the impulse to race after her. He wanted to follow her wherever she went and get far more than the brief taste he'd just had of her. Somewhere along the way, his brain completely stopped functioning as he drove her back to her car. When he felt her lush curves against his arm when he stopped for the deer, his body simply took over. Even now, after kneeling on the icy road to change her tire, his body was barely in check. His cock was so hard, it was uncomfortable to sit. He *never* lost control the way he'd come close to with her. Somehow, his conscience tapped on his shoulder and offered just enough discipline that he managed to stop. When she sat on his lap, he could feel the wet heat of her against his cock through his jeans. Her breasts, generous and near perfect with rosy nipples, had almost pushed him over the edge. The way she was in his arms, tentative and bold at once without an ounce of calculation in her, wild with passion—he didn't know how he'd managed to stop.

He thought of her eyes—that uncertainty, as if she couldn't believe what he was saying —and wondered. It was hard to imagine she hadn't been fawned over before. While he couldn't say they'd been close before, he knew her to mostly keep to herself. She had the wild, sexy edge that female shifters had, even if she kept it shrouded behind her quiet, unassuming manner. He rolled down his window, icy air whipping through the truck, in an effort to cool the fire she'd started in his body. By the time he got home, he was shivering and had managed to get rid of the bulge in his pants.

When he walked into his mother's house, he found her sitting in the kitchen, her face tired and gaunt. She'd always been a thin woman and had only gotten thinner since she'd been sick. He knew the chemo treatments wore on her. His heart tightened, but he shoved down the fear and pain waiting in the wings. He didn't want her to die and didn't want to face the possibility.

"Hey Mom. How're you feeling?"

She glanced up from whatever she was reading, a soft smile gracing her face. She shrugged gently. "As well as could be expected. Did you take care of Lily's tire?"

While he'd waited with his mother at her chemo appointment, he'd shared his encounter with Lily that morning. A hot flush rose when he considered what transpired other than changing Lily's tire. "Yup. All taken care of."

His mother nodded approvingly and went back to reading. Since he'd moved back home to help her, he'd come to learn she savored quiet. He didn't ask her about it, but it was such a marked contrast from his home when he was a boy he could only guess she appreciated the absence of noise his father had constantly created. When his father was alive, there was either a television blaring, or he was barking about something or other. Now that it had been over a decade since Noah had moved out, he'd had time to consider his father. Willis had been a restless, unhappy soul. Noah surmised that the constant thrum of background noise kept Willis from thinking too much. Willis had despised the secrecy around shifters and was known to rant about how stupid it was when they could easily overpower humans if needed.

His mother had offered little about what she knew of his father's background. Noah knew they'd married young when Carol got pregnant when she was only seventeen. She wasn't a shifter, but came from a family known to be friendly toward shifters. Willis had been raised by a man much like himself, so it stood to reason he repeated the pattern. When Noah contemplated his mother's influence on him, he couldn't put words to how thankful he was for her influence. By happenstance he had a mother who taught him there were possibilities beyond useless rage even though she faced it almost daily when his father was alive.

His mother startled him by speaking again. "I heard today they're coordinating with the police out in Montana. One of the nurses at the hospital told me about it. She only had secondhand information, but said rumor was they're hoping to get Theo to talk." Carol sighed and lifted her eyes to him. "You could help them, you know. With your military experience..."

"Mom, you keep saying that, but..."

She cut him off. "But what? You're a good boy, always have been. You act like no one in Catamount will trust you because of your father and his family. I think you only make it worse by keeping to yourself. I'm happier than I can say to have you home. I hope you want to stay no matter what happens to me. I might not be a shifter, but I know it's not easy being who you are when you're not in a place like Catamount."

He closed his eyes and took a breath. His mother was right and he knew it, but he needed some time to get his bearings again. Catamount was home, but he was still figuring out how to reconcile the boy he'd been when he left to the man he'd become after years in the Special Forces. A part of him sincerely wanted to offer his help on the investigation since Callen's death, but he didn't want to ruffle any feathers. He opened his eyes and found his mother waiting patiently. "Maybe I'll stop by Jake North's office again tomorrow."

His mother, sensible as she was, didn't

push any more. She simply nodded and went back to reading. Hours later, Noah lay in bed, his mind and body replaying those heated moments with Lily. He kicked the covers off and strode to the bathroom. Even after a hot shower and a quick, completely unsatisfying self-induced release, he failed to quell the lust that surged through him when Lily sashayed through his thoughts.

"IF YOU WERE HOPING to hide your thing with Noah, you might want to stop making out on the side of the road," Roxanne said quietly, her eyes sly.

Lily couldn't keep her mouth from falling open. When Roxanne chuckled at the look on her face, Lily snapped her mouth shut and groaned, her face heating up. "Where did you hear that?" she hedged.

They were sitting on the couch at Phoebe's house. By chance, they were the only two in the room. Phoebe and Shana were in the kitchen, and Chloe had stepped into the bathroom. Phoebe frequently hosted girls' nights where they shared din-ner, occasionally played cards, or watched whatever suited their fancy on television. Shana's late husband happened to be Callen Peyton, the shifter who'd died in mountain lion form on a highway and left a trail of secrets behind him. Since his death a few months back, they hadn't had a girls' night together. In the ensuing months, Chloe had fallen in love with Dane and joined their small circle. Nice as it was to finally get together, the current of turmoil among Catamount shifters ran under every moment.

Phoebe poked her head into the living room. "More wine?"

Roxanne reached for the bottle on the coffee table, testing its weight. "No, we're good for now."

Phoebe disappeared back into the kitchen, and Roxanne turned back to Lily. "I didn't hear it from anyone. I drove past your car on my way home and saw Noah's windows steamed up like it was nobody's business. It's not like I could really see anything, but I'm not stupid."

Lily took a gulp of wine and finally managed to look at Roxanne. "There is no 'thing' with us. He..." She paused, her face hot. *He made me feel things I've never felt and made me so desperate for more, I can't stop thinking about him.*

Roxanne's eyes softened. "Just teasing, you know. I already told you I think Noah's a good guy. He happens to be sexy as hell too."

Lily couldn't help the giggle that escaped. "No argument from me on that point. When I said there's no thing, it's just 'cause all that happened was he kissed me. I don't know what it means."

Roxanne twirled her wineglass, watching the rich red wine swirl before she looked up again, her eyes thoughtful. "Did he say anything?"

Lily chewed the inside of her mouth and shrugged. "He said he wanted to get to know me."

Roxanne's smiled slowly. "Well, then that's what it means."

Lily wanted to scream. *That's what it means? I need more to understand. What does getting to know me mean? What happens after that? And then...Shut up.* Again, an off switch would be so helpful for her brain. Still blushing, Lily looked up when Chloe came out of the bathroom. Chloe had only been in Catamount for a few months, though it appeared she was here to stay. Dane had claimed her so fast, it made Lily's head spin and made her wonder how come she'd never had that kind of an effect on a man. Chloe glanced between Lily and Roxanne, her gaze curious. "I'm gonna see if they need any help in the kitchen," she offered as she walked past them into the kitchen.

Lily turned back to Roxanne. "You know I'm terrible at relationships," she said bluntly.

Roxanne rolled her eyes. "You can't say you're terrible at something you've never even tried. Noah wouldn't have said anything if he didn't mean it. He's never been known as a guy to play around."

Lily returned the eye roll. "Since when did you become an expert on him? He's only been back in town a few months."

Roxanne took a sip of wine and chuckled. "Maybe so, but I know his mom. Plus, I don't think he even dated anyone in high school. He kept to himself. His mother would love for him to give someone a chance. She worries he's too focused on taking care of her. But..." Roxanne paused and practically glared at Lily. "You are an absolute master at avoiding relationships and acting like it's because no one bothers to notice you. You're cute as hell and plenty of men have noticed, but you keep getting in your own way."

Sometimes Roxanne's blunt observations and advice were appreciated, and sometimes they weren't. At the moment, Lily crossed and uncrossed her legs, took another gulp of wine and tried to figure out how to ignore Roxanne's point. Roxanne might be right, but no one knew Lily's avoidance of relationships had mushroomed the older she got and the longer she stayed a virgin. Her entire life she'd struggled to figure out how to make sense of the way she was. She liked people, but only in small doses. By the time high school and then college came and went, she discovered the quick connections many people made didn't come easily to her. She was an introvert, which didn't fit too well in the fast-paced social world. Another layer to the complication were her conflicted feelings about being a shifter. Sometimes, all she wanted was to be a plain human and fall in love with just a man. The only sparks she'd ever felt though were with shifters. Noah was in his own category, but still. As far as relationships went, it wasn't as if she'd never dated, only that it had been rare and her anxiety reliably got in the way. If Noah hadn't surprised her so much today, she would have bet his kiss never would have happened.

She sighed and met Roxanne's eyes. "Maybe you're right. No matter what, I'm not exactly up to speed with interpreting men's intentions."

Roxanne looped an arm over Lily's shoulders. "How about you practice not avoiding Noah for a start?"

Lily had just taken a sip of wine and almost spit it out. When she caught her breath, she glanced at Roxanne whose eyes were bright. "Wow! You don't ask for much, do you? I suppose I could start with that," she said wryly.

Phoebe called out that dinner was ready. Roxanne and Lily made their way into the kitchen. After dinner and two rounds of rummy, Jake arrived while they were still lounging around the kitchen table. Phoebe was standing by the sink rinsing dishes. Jake slipped his arms around her waist and dropped a lingering kiss in the curve of her neck. Lily happened to look their way and caught an intimate glance between them. Her eyes bounced off of them, and she sighed as conversation continued around her. She was beyond thrilled her brother had finally (*finally!*) allowed himself to love Phoebe the way he'd denied himself for years. She didn't like to think about it, but it made her feel a little lonely. They'd never spoken of it, but she'd felt a tiny kinship with Phoebe. Though Phoebe had dated more than Lily had when they were younger, she'd never been too serious with anyone, most likely because her unexpressed love for Jake was a pretty big obstacle. Happy as Lily was for her brother and Phoebe to find their way to each other, she was starting to feel more and more like something wasn't quite right with her.

As she drove home through the cold, dark night a little while later, she wondered when she'd see Noah again.

5

———————

Noah took a swallow of Roxanne's coffee and pushed through the door outside. Catamount had been graced with another foot of snow during the night. The sun broke through the clouds in spots, leaving glittering paths in its light as the snow melted. He stepped over a snow bank and walked across the road to his truck. While he waited for his truck to warm up, another truck pulled alongside him. When he saw the driver's side window open, he rolled down his window to find Derek Miller. Derek's dark blonde hair curled out from under the hat he wore. Derek's blue eyes were slightly guarded, but he looked determined. Noah waited for him to speak.

Derek cleared his throat. "You got a few minutes?"

Noah nodded, his mind turning over what Derek might want to discuss. "Sure. What's up?"

Derek shifted his shoulders. "I could use some advice and thought maybe you'd be a good one to ask."

"Why's that?"

Derek's eyes held his for a moment. "I'm sure you guessed there's a reason Kirk wanted to haul off and punch me. With everything going on, I'm not sure who's safe to talk to, but I think you might be because you got my back the other day."

Noah's curiosity was piqued. "Can't say I blame you for wondering who's safe to talk to. Shit's hittin' the fan left and right around here. After Theo got arrested, I figured I'd better lay low. I can't even remember the last time I talked to him, but he's my uncle, so..."

Derek waved his hand dismissively. "Man, everyone knows you had hardly anything to do with your dad's family. Not sayin' that to be a jerk, that's just how it is."

Noah recalled his mother's comment yesterday and wondered if she was more right than he'd given her credit for. He met Derek's gaze and nodded. "I guess that's good to know."

Derek started to say something when a couple passed on the sidewalk nearby. "You mind meeting me out at my office?"

Noah curiosity went from mild to serious, but he nodded. He and Derek hadn't been buddy-buddy in high school, but they'd hung out a few times. Given his family life, Noah didn't ever have anyone over when his father was alive, so the semi-friendship he'd had with Derek all those years ago was par for the course. After a short drive, he followed Derek down the road that led into one of the quarries owned by his family. The main office for their stone and construction business was located here. Once they were inside, Derek got right to the point.

"I should probably go straight to the police with this. I can't believe I'm about to say this, but I'm kinda scared. I figured maybe you'd be a good one to talk to because no one around here would try to screw with you. He'll never admit it, but Kirk's not gonna take you on after the other day. It's not like much happened, but that's exactly it. You stopped him cold."

"If you think you should go to the police,

you should probably go to the police." Noah stated the obvious.

Derek tugged his hat off and flung it on a chair beside the desk. "I know. It's not so easy when it involves someone who used to be my friend."

Noah leaned against the wall by the door and waited. It was obvious Derek wanted to spill whatever he was worried about, so Noah figured all he had to do was wait.

Derek sighed and rested his hips against the desk, crossing his arms. "Kirk wants access to one of our quarries further out of town. If you hadn't heard elsewhere, I had to fire him a few years back. Until then, we were pretty good friends. I knew he had some issues with partying too hard, but I didn't know how far things had gone until I tried to help him out with a job. He goofed off, hardly ever showed up and expected to get paid anyway. I don't know if he's held a job for more than a few months at a time. Anyway, last week he showed up out here with Callen's brother, Brad. He didn't out and out threaten me, but it was pretty damn clear if I didn't agree to let them have access to the quarry, they'd make life difficult for me. When you saw us at Roxanne's deli the other day, I invited him to lunch to tell him to fuck off. Since then, Brad's truck has shown up out at the quarry twice. It may be remote, but we have security cameras installed. Too many problems with yahoos wanting to cliff dive and shit like that. My best guess is Brad and Kirk are in deep with the smuggling bullshit and they need a remote location for deliveries."

Derek paused and took a deep breath. "What the hell should I do?"

"You already know what you should do. Go to the police." Noah was of two minds. Part of him wanted to walk out of here and pretend he'd never heard any of this. But a much bigger part of him wanted to dive in and root out whoever else was involved. Catamount had always been a safe stronghold for shifters, but now it was in serious danger.

Derek kicked his heel against the steel desk, the sound reverberating in the small room. "Problem is, I keep getting these weird texts from a number I don't recognize about making sure I do what I need to do to keep my daughter safe. If anything happened to Jasmine, I'd lose it."

Jasmine was Derek's daughter from a

young marriage. His wife had died in a car accident, and Derek had raised Jasmine on his own since then. Noah's gut didn't like any of this. At all.

"How old is Jasmine now?"

"Twelve going on twenty. She's a good kid. If you told me Kirk would get so in deep with this shit, he'd threaten her, I'd have said you were crazy. But I don't know anymore. I don't know if he's blowing smoke up my ass just to get me to shut my mouth, or what. After they kidnapped Chloe though, I'm not dumb enough to take chances. I know I should just go straight to Hank Anderson, but if they find out I did, I don't know what they'll do."

Hank Anderson was Catamount's police chief and a shifter. Noah unfortunately knew him better than he'd like due to his father's propensity to get caught up in petty legal issues when Noah had been growing up. "I'll talk to Hank. Can't promise they won't try to blame you, but at least you don't have to lie when you say it wasn't you."

"You'd do that?"

Noah shrugged. "Yeah. No sweat off my back. I may have been gone for years, but I hate seeing what's happened in Catamount since Callen died and everything blew up. This used to be the one place I felt safe being a shifter. It pisses me off they'd threaten your daughter. She's a kid! I'll stop by the police station this afternoon. If they want to talk to you about it, they can call and you don't have to worry about being seen down there for now."

Derek nodded. "Right. It's not like Kirk hasn't already put me in a hell of a position. All I meant to do was ask for some advice, but I'm beyond thankful you're willing to help out like this. If you change your mind..."

Noah shook his head sharply. "Won't happen. I'm headed there now. I'll call you."

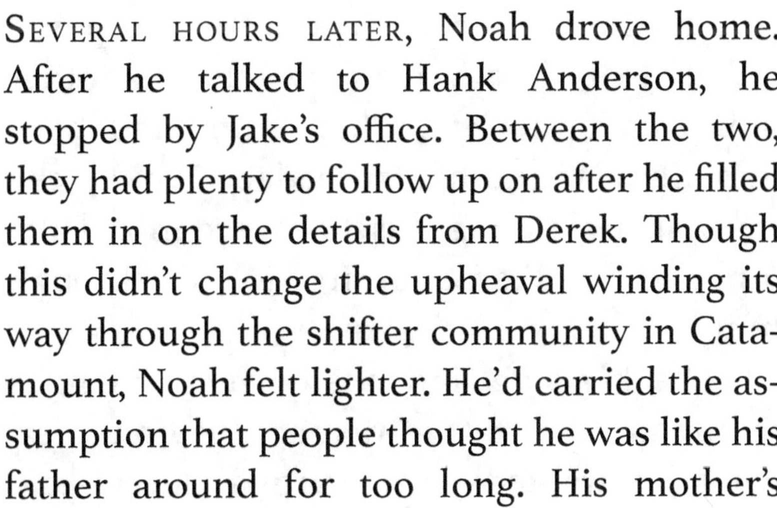

SEVERAL HOURS LATER, Noah drove home. After he talked to Hank Anderson, he stopped by Jake's office. Between the two, they had plenty to follow up on after he filled them in on the details from Derek. Though this didn't change the upheaval winding its way through the shifter community in Catamount, Noah felt lighter. He'd carried the assumption that people thought he was like his father around for too long. His mother's point and today's interactions had shown him it wasn't as simple as he'd thought. If anything, he supposed he should have known how it looked that he'd stayed out of Catamount until after his father died.

After he got home, he headed into the woods behind his mother's house for a run. He was still getting used to the fact that he could disappear into the woods and let his mountain lion run free. Once he was out of sight, he shifted. In a flash, heat prickled under his skin and fur rippled across the surface. He stretched and took off running, bounding through the deep snow into the foothills. It was close to dusk, but he had enough light to stretch and flex his cat for a little while. As he circled back toward his mother's property, he saw a flash of tawny gold in the distance. He came to a stop and quietly leapt into a tree to watch. In another moment, a mountain lion wandered back into view. As the lion threaded through the trees at a slow jog, his lion recognized the other—Lily. Fierce desire jolted through him.

The blessing and challenge in being a mountain lion shifter was that his lion knew what he wanted—on a primal level—and was definitive. If his lion didn't have to wrestle with his human conscience, he'd leap down from the tree and bound after Lily. In cat form, she was lithe and beautiful. Suddenly, she came to a stop. He knew she sensed his presence. Her tail flicked, its black tip visible in the fading light. In the quiet of winter dusk, her eyes found his. An owl called softly in the distance as they watched each other. Noah leapt down from his perch and stood in the snow. Lily's eyes were bright blue, pinned to him through the snowy quiet of the forest. The pulse of desire between them was so powerful, he could feel its reverberations in the air. She lifted her chin, her tail flicking once more, before she turned and sauntered off.

Noah had to call upon every ounce of restraint to keep from racing after her. He clung to the reason provided by his humanity and watched and waited until she was out of sight. He raced through the woods until he got home, shifting before he stepped out of the trees. After a shower, he checked on his mother. She was sound asleep with a book fallen on her chest. He picked up the book and marked the page before setting it quietly on the nightstand. When he returned to the kitchen to scrounge up dinner, his phone buzzed. He was startled to see a text from Lily on the screen. He'd gotten her number yesterday after he'd finished changing her tire.

Can I see you?

Noah didn't know what he'd expected, but it wasn't this. His pulse pounded as he held his phone in hand. Before he had a chance to reply, another text flashed on the screen.

Okay, maybe that was weird.

He realized he'd better reply before she changed her mind.

Yes. Tonight? Not weird.

His phone remained quiet with no return text for enough long moments that Noah wondered if she'd changed her mind. His body was running on high idle after the brief encounter in the woods. He was rummaging through the kitchen cabinet when his phone buzzed again.

Dinner at The Trailhead? Half hour?

Her directness surprised him, but he wasn't about to say no. He shot off a quick confirmation and grabbed his truck keys.

6

───────

Lily stared at herself in the bathroom mirror. Her golden brown hair fell in soft waves around her shoulders. She wasn't one to spend much time on her hair, which is why she generally left it loose. Even the nerve rattling prospect of dinner with Noah couldn't bring her to know what else to do with it. She added a touch of eyeliner and lip gloss and threw on her winter jacket on the way through the living room. She lived alone in a small house on the outskirts of Catamount. She'd bought this house mostly because she was enchanted with its design. It was an octagon home with a wide open living room and kitchen area in the main part of the home and windows on every wall. A single bedroom and bathroom were to the side with laundry and a guest room and bathroom in the lower floor. She loved the skylight at the center of the roof where the angles came together.

She hit the remote starter for her car and waited by the windows. The moon was close to full tonight, its silvery light bathing the trees, making the night seem magical. Her pulse was thrumming and had been ever since she'd seen Noah in the woods this afternoon. Seeing him in lion form, her cat had known, beyond a doubt, that she had to have him. She wanted him like she'd never wanted anyone. Part of her chafed at this. Her conflicted feelings about being a shifter came, in part, from how irrational the lion side of her was. Her human half relished logic, order and reason. She hated admitting it, but she knew part of the reason she struggled with being a shifter was the intensity of emotion, the primal quality of the experience. It made her feel out of control, like she couldn't quite rein herself in. Today, seeing Noah in the woods was all feeling, all drive. After she shifted, it occurred to her that maybe she could use that drive to get over the side of herself that stood in the way of relationships. Or more specifically, left her stuck being a virgin even though it annoyed her to no end.

Impulsively, she decided she would see him tonight and, instead of hemming and hawing, she'd just do what her body wanted and have him. She was determined to lose her pesky virginity once and for all. While half of her thought she was flat out of her mind, the other half of her knew if she let herself wait, she'd get in her own way. As she always had. She wanted so much more than those heated moments in his truck. Tension drew her tight, but desire strummed through her.

The only problem she couldn't find a way around was how to tell him she was a virgin. It seemed like she should, but she didn't know. She was worried he'd think something was wrong with her. She sure as hell did. Every time she tried to date someone her brain got in the way. She figured if she didn't do something drastic, she'd get more stuck than she already was. With a sigh, she checked her watch and headed out.

When she arrived at The Trailhead, she saw Noah's truck already in the parking lot. The Trailhead was located in an old-style diner building with shiny stainless steel on the outside and a bright red roof. The inside of the café retained the diner feel with a counter facing an open kitchen and scattered tables and booths. Cheery paint colors and arts shared space on the walls with photos of through-hikers of the Appalachian Trail and faded newspaper photos of mountain lions. The Trailhead served down-home diner fare with upscale healthy and gourmet meals. Maine had long been a tourist attraction to the city dwellers along the Eastern seaboard. By extension, it had become a destination for good food with the entire state scattered with excellent restaurants. Catamount had their share with The Trailhead a local favorite.

Lily spied Noah seated at a booth. Her mind conjured the memory of his mountain lion in the forest today. He was tall and majestic, his amber eyes almost electric when he caught hers. She'd had to battle with herself, the pull to him had been so strong. Simply looking at him now, her heart started racing and desire unfurled through her veins, flushing her skin. She caught the hostess's eye and gestured toward Noah before she began walking in his direction. He looked up, his eyes instantly locking with hers. Across the restaurant, she felt the burn of his gaze.

Somehow, she managed to sit down across from him in the booth. Her pulse danced, and her breath was shallow. Heat suffused her. A waitress came by to take their drink order. The momentary activity gave her a chance to gather her wits. After a few minutes of casual conversation, Noah commented that he stopped by Jake's office today.

"You did?" Noah generally kept to himself, so hearing he stopped by her brother's office seemed out of the ordinary.

"Yup. Remember that little incident between Derek and Kirk at Roxanne's store the other day?" At her nod, he continued. "Derek and I were kind of friends in high school. To make a long story short, he asked me for some advice because Kirk's been on him about getting access to one of his quarries out of town. Best guess is they're hoping to use it for deliveries somewhere remote. Kirk came to ask him about it with Callen's brother, Brad. I offered to talk to Hank Anderson about it and stopped by to chat with Jake after that."

Lily stared at him. She hadn't known what she expected from him, but it wasn't this. She was relieved he'd gone straight to Hank with the information, but the niggling fear she carried just wouldn't go away lately. Since Jake was working on the investigation around Callen's death and the smuggling network, she'd probably heard more than most about the many leads they'd chased down. It felt like every time they tied up one loose end, another unraveled. She took a breath. "I'm glad you went straight to the police with it. I didn't know you and Derek were friends."

Noah shrugged. "He's as much of a friend as anyone in Catamount. With the way my dad was, not too many people came around. Derek and I hung out a little. I didn't see anything to do other than talk to Hank about it. This whole thing's just a mess. More and more, I wonder if Callen's father is also involved. Jake said he's been wondering the same thing."

The conversation moved on. Lily was relieved not to dwell on the investigation. She was weary from having it dominate every conversation. Noah had ordered a bottle of wine. Sometime after they finished eating, she realized she'd more than helped herself to the wine. She chalked it up to her nerves and how ridiculously distracting Noah was. Every time he turned those dark amber eyes to her, her pulse skittered and wet heat built inside. She remembered the promise she'd made to herself—she wouldn't get in her own way tonight.

When they stood up to leave, Noah glanced at her. "How about I drive you home?"

For a moment, she considered arguing, but she knew she might have had too much to drink, and if she let him drive her home, she might not chicken out. At her nod, he walked at her side on the way out, his palm coming to rest in her low back. The heat of his subtle touch burned into her skin, spiraling heat outward through her. Noah's truck was running and warm when they got to it. The luxury of remote start was downright amazing in the cold winters of Maine. Lily sat beside Noah in the truck, the memory of the last time she'd been in here flashing like neon lights in her brain. As he drove the short drive toward her house, desire and anxiety warred within her. The space between them felt minute and immense at once. She glanced at his profile— his chiseled features and sensual mouth stirring the sparks of heat burning inside of her.

She managed to guide him through the few turns to her home. When he pulled up, she thought she might die if he didn't kiss her again. It was all she wanted. He turned to look at her, and she gathered every ounce of nerve she could find.

"Do you want to come in?" she blurted out.

She couldn't read his dark gaze, but he nodded, so she didn't stop and think. She climbed out of his truck and strode quickly to the door. She was still fumbling with her keys when he caught up with her. Her nerves and the cold were making her hands shake. Suddenly, Noah's warmth surrounded her as he brought his arm around her from behind and closed his hand over hers.

"Easy," he said, his voice low and gruff at her ear.

He steadied her hand, and she finally managed to get the key in the lock and turn it. Once they stepped inside, she turned on a few lamps. Noah stood in the center of the circular room looking up into the skylight. Snow had started to fall on the drive to her house. It drifted like stardust against the skylight.

He dropped his gaze and glanced around the room. "Nice place."

She shrugged. "Thanks. I like it."

She could hardly contain the desire rushing through her in waves. She broke away from his eyes and stepped to the door to hang her jacket on the coat rack. She toed her boots off and turned to find him right behind her, his jacket hooked over his finger. Without a word, she took it and hung it beside hers. In the silence, she tried to think of all the possible things she could say, but all that was in her mind was the tug to get close to him. It was purely visceral. Coasting on the depth of her desire, the flicker of feeling her lion held onto pushed her forward. She took one step and felt the heat of his body against hers. She heard the sharp intake of his breath and didn't stop to think.

She placed her hand on the center of his chest and stroked up, savoring the beat of his heart under her palm, and slid her hand around the back of his neck, threading into his dark curls. With a soft tug, she leaned up. He met her halfway. The feel of his mouth against hers sent a jolt through her system.

On her gasp, he took over, his tongue sweeping into her mouth. They tumbled right back to where they'd been the other afternoon. Only this time, the heat built so rapidly, she shuddered at its intensity. His arms came around her, and he lifted her easily.

She heard two thumps, his boots hitting the floor behind them as he stepped away from the door. His lips never broke from hers as he hooked an arm under her hips and carried her to the sofa. Next thing she knew, she was piled in his lap and she couldn't get close enough. Their kiss went from a slow, deep exploration to wild and wet. She scrambled over him, straddling his hips, gasping at the feel of his hard shaft against her. Once again, whatever it was between them simply took over and wiped her mind clean. She didn't worry about what was going to happen next like she usually did. Sensation drove her, spurring her on.

Noah tore his lips from hers in a groan. He pulled back just far enough to meet her eyes. What she saw in his brought a hard tug inside of her. He threaded a hand in her hair, his thumb stroking softly at her nape. Every little touch sent sparks sizzling along her skin. He swore softly and took a shuddering breath before bringing his lips to hers again. A hot, deep kiss and his lips dusted across her cheek to trace her ear. Hot shivers chased in the wake of his touch. He stroked down her back before sliding up under her shirt, the calloused skin of his palms eliciting a groan.

Lily moved restlessly against him, sharp pinwheels of pleasure rolling through her every time she pressed down against his hard cock. She tugged at his shirt, pushing it up his chest. He leaned forward, easily adjusting her weight in his lap, and pulled his shirt up and off in a quick motion. It fell in an arc as he tossed it. His other hand stayed busy, deftly unhooking her bra before sliding both hands up her sides. She followed the motion of his hands as they coasted up her sides and drew her arms up, her shirt following. She sighed in relief when her breasts tumbled out as he tossed her bra to the side. The contrast of his muscled chest and rock-hard abs against the softness of her breasts sent a shudder through her.

Noah pushed her back slightly, his hands curling under her breasts. He met her eyes, his dark with need. Without a word passing between them, Lily knew he wanted her as much as she wanted him. Her mind, so practiced at self-doubt, tried to speak up, but her body knew better in the thick of this moment and ignored it. His eyes tracked over her face and down to her breasts, feeding air to the fire twisting inside of her. Restless, she shifted against him, sliding her hands up his muscled chest.

He thumbed her nipples. A liquid hot shiver rippled through her as she arched into his touch. Desire spun tightly around them. His eyes flicked back up to hers, a question in them. Though her mind had taken a backseat to her body, a flicker of conscience nudged her. She had to tell him she was a virgin. With one hand cupping a breast, toying with her nipple, he slid the other up coasting across her neck and lacing into her hair. His thumb brushed the pulse beat in her neck. His eyes darkened before he fit his mouth over hers in a devouring kiss. Her senses scrambled as she gasped into his mouth. Sensation teemed, desire thundering through her. He drew back, his lips, tongue and teeth traveling down her neck. Tight and achy everywhere, she strained to get closer. Want coiled tighter and tighter inside as he brought his relentless lips to her breasts, drawing first one and then other into his mouth, the moist suction driving her wild.

Pleasure streaked through her when he groaned against her, his teeth closing around her nipple in a sharp bite. Desperate for more, she pushed her hips back and tore at the buttons of his jeans. Noah lips went still, and he slowly pulled back. In the quiet, the air fairly sizzled between them. His eyes were like hot embers. He traced lazy circles around her nipples as he beheld her.

"What do you want?" he asked, his words rough and raw.

Lily flushed, but held his gaze. "You. This."

He nodded slowly. "I saw you today."

She knew he spoke of when he saw her in the woods. She recalled the moment she noticed him waiting in the trees. Her mountain lion didn't doubt what she felt between them. The thread between them vibrated when she locked eyes with him in the forest. The part of her beyond thought and reason knew he was to be hers, and she to be his in that flicker.

Noah's hand tightened in her hair though

he remained silent. She knew he was waiting for her.

"I saw you too." Her words fell in a raw whisper. The intimacy between them was almost too much. She'd never experienced this, but somehow she couldn't turn from it. Her emotions tossed like a kite in the wind. Her very being strained for him while the weak voice of reason reminded her it was only fair to tell him she was a virgin. No matter the power of connection she felt, no matter that she'd known the look she saw in his lion's eyes when he stared at her through the snowy trees, branding her with his look, she couldn't go into this without being honest. The self-doubt that had created worn paths in her mind reared its ugly head, reminding her Noah likely thought she was a wild, sexy shifter who'd had plenty of experience with men. She didn't want to let him down, didn't want him to pull away.

Her eyes fell, landing on his chest, a sight to behold. Most mountain lion shifters were incredible physical specimens. Noah was no exception, unless one counted that he'd adhered to rigorous training standards for the Marines Special Forces. He was all muscle, coiled and conditioned. She took a shuddering breath and gathered her courage. When she met his eyes, her words came out like a shot. "I'm a virgin."

His eyes widened, but he didn't move. His hand stayed laced in her hair, his thumb kept up its idle strokes on the soft skin under her ear and neck, brushing back and forth over her pulse. Her heart beat wildly, but she managed to keep her chin up. After a long moment, he spoke. "Wouldn't have guessed that." He fell silent again, his eyes considering.

Pressure built within her, the need to explain, to make sense of it. She somehow felt apologetic. It was inconvenient and added a layer of complication. She didn't know what Noah wanted. "I thought I should say something. I ended up this way because..." She paused and shrugged, feeling somewhat ridiculous given that she was half naked and could still feel the heated length of him against her core, which was drenched with want. "Because I'm not so good at the casual, fun thing. I'm not a prude about sex or anything. It wasn't like I was saving myself. It just..."

"You don't have to explain, Lily."

She took a breath. Her mind was distracted from its tendency toward rumination with the soft strokes of his thumb and the burn of his amber eyes.

"Does that change anything for you?" he asked.

She knew what he meant. She couldn't quite believe it, but when he watched her in the woods, she knew he meant to claim her. It was as simple as that—a primal knowledge supported solely by feelings only her mountain lion side could have convinced her to be true. Conflicted though she may be at times by her shared self—lion and human—it was who she was. She shook her head. "Does it change anything for you?"

His mouth curled into the slightest smile when he shook his head. His gaze sobered. "It only makes me want you more. It wouldn't have mattered either way, but I won't pretend it doesn't feel good knowing no one else knows you that way." He paused and held her eyes. The air around them felt alive. She could barely breathe as desire pulsed through her. "Maybe we should slow down though."

"No!" She shook her head forcefully, determined not to let what was unfolding stop. She'd finally gotten the courage to kick her anxiety to the curb long enough to get through the worst of it. She wasn't about to deny herself what she wanted.

She moved abruptly, pushing back to tear his jeans open. He started to say something, but his words ended in a groan when she curled her hands around his cock. The warm velvety skin pulsed against her hands as she stroked up and down. Noah's breath hissed through his teeth before he caught her hands in his and lifted her in his arms as he stood suddenly. He glanced around before his eyes landed on her again. "Bedroom?" His voice was ragged, his features taut.

Euphoria crested inside as she realized he likely wasn't putting the brakes on this just because she was a virgin. She gestured to the door to one side of the circular room, and he strode quickly over. Though she was short, she had generous curves, but he held her with ease, juggling his hold on her when he needed to open the door. Her bed was piled high with pillows and a luxurious down quilt.

Noah headed straight for the bed. He set her down on it and stood. She moved to kneel, but he moved swiftly. He stretched atop her, his elbows bracketing her face. He leaned up briefly to flick on the single lamp beside her bed, his weight settling against her again. The feel of him above her amped the desire thrumming through her. "If we're doing this, you're following my lead." His words were gruff, his gaze heated.

She nodded wordlessly. He didn't wait and brought his mouth to hers. In seconds, she spiraled back to the place she'd been— the place where nothing but feeling reigned. His kisses drove her mad—slow, hot, wet, and drugging. By the time he tore his lips away, she was panting, her body on fire. His lips made their way down her neck to her breasts. The moments that followed spun her tighter and tighter in the grip of desire. Broken gasps fell from her lips. Sweet pressure gathered inside as she chased after the ecstasy his touch promised. He mapped her body with his mouth and hands, his touch everywhere at once. He traced her navel with his tongue, dusting kisses over the soft curve of her abdomen as he deftly unbuttoned her jeans and dragged them down. She lifted her hips, frantic for more.

She was slick with desire and wanted to feel him inside of her. *Now.* But he wasn't to be hurried. Her hoarse pleas were answered with his hands and mouth. He left her panties on, a scrap of blue silk, as his lips made their way down her legs. He trailed his fingers along the inside of her thighs and behind the soft skin of her knees. After her jeans were tossed aside, he made his way back up. By the time he cupped his palm over her mound, she was awash in a tumult of sensation, spun so tight with desire, she was near out of her mind.

He stroked across the wet silk between her thighs. She arched into him, desperate for more. Only after excruciating moments of teasing, stroking her slowly, coasting over her clit through the silk, did he finally hook his finger over the edge of her panties and yank them down. He moved on to dragging his fingers back and forth through her slick folds, teasing her to near madness before finally sliding a finger inside her channel. She was so close to orgasm, her channel throbbed around him. He stroked in and out of her slowly, adding another finger and then his mouth. Liquid heat suffused her as she careened into sensation. With a deep surge of his fingers, he drew her clit into his mouth, and sharp pleasure burst through her as she shuddered around him. He didn't stop until her hips stilled. His lips retraced the path they'd taken down her body, making their way up in a leisurely manner. His warmth left her. Dazed, she opened her eyes to see him kicking his jeans off.

Seeing him bare took her breath away. He was hard, honed muscle from head to toe. She'd gotten a sense of it, but the size of him sobered her. She wasn't quite so sure how he'd manage to fit inside of her. Her desire for Noah went so far beyond anything she'd experienced, she couldn't even contemplate stopping, but a flicker of anxiety coursed through her. His dark eyes locked on her as he rolled a condom on. In a smooth movement, he stretched across her, his elbows again bracketing her face. His expression was tight, as if he was exerting great control. She felt the head of his cock nudge at her entrance. On the heels of the single most intense orgasm she'd ever experienced, desire pricked at her, that heavy, wet ache between her legs arching toward him.

His eyes coasted over her face as if he was searching for something. He brushed her tangled hair away before bringing his lips to hers again. Noah's kisses stole her senses, stirred her thoughts away and narrowed the world to only the feeling of him—the hard planes of his body against hers. She dragged her hands down his back, savoring the corded muscles under her hands. He nudged against her entrance, the tease of his touch notching her higher and higher. Once again, he brought her closer and closer to ecstasy. She arched her hips into his, gasping when he nipped her neck. In a swift move, he surged deeply inside of her. For a split second, pain sliced through her. He held completely still, but didn't pull back. She opened her eyes to find his trained on hers. Just as quickly, the pain started to dissipate as her body adjusted to his fullness. Her breath came back and the tension eased from her.

Only then did he begin to move in slow strokes. His eyes fell closed again, hers following. Everything narrowed to the feel of him surging inside her. The burn of his entrance faded, and she arched into him, meeting his strokes. A different pleasure built, this one deeper, hungrier. Her nails scored his back as she danced along the delicious edge. Her climax unfurled slowly this time, the sweet pressure starting in her channel as she throbbed around him, and then spiking when he slid his hand between them, his thumb circling over her clit. She tumbled over, savoring the fullness inside her as she clenched him. His hips drummed against hers rapidly before he cried out and fell against her.

He brought his weight to the side, so he didn't crush her. Their ragged breathing slowed in unison. Lily finally opened her eyes and rolled her head to the side. Noah opened his eyes when she turned. His head rested on his elbow in the pillows while his other hand had landed under the curve of her breast. He lifted his hand and brushed her hair out of her face. It was a wild tangle. She giggled and was rewarded with a smile from him.

They lay like that for a while, quiet. She considered how she felt, but for once in her life, she managed not to let her mind climb on its hamster wheel of worry and wondering. He stroked his hand down her arm and finally lifted his hips, slowly pulling out of her. She started to protest, but he shook his head.

"You're cold. I'll be right back."

He stood and stepped into the bathroom adjacent to her bedroom. She heard water running before he returned. He'd disposed of his condom and had a warm washcloth in hand. She flushed all over when he carefully wiped her before tossing the washcloth in the sink. Her body was a mix of lethargy and humming energy. Noah chuckled when he tried to tug the quilt from underneath her. After a temporary tug of war, he lifted the quilt high, the rush of air a contrast to the furnace of his body when he climbed in bed beside her.

His gaze sobered as he tucked her against his side. "So..."

She eyed him. "Don't make me talk. Can we just enjoy the moment?" She didn't have it in her to try to process what happened aloud. She didn't know if it was possible, but she didn't want to let the wheels in her brain start turning too fast.

A dark brow arched up. After a brief silence, he shrugged. "Sure. I can stay for a little bit, but I have to go home to check on my mom."

Her heart clenched. He'd gone and blown her mind tonight. She was so stirred up physically and emotionally, she could hardly think clearly, and he had to go and remind her why he was so much more than just handsome and sexy as hell. She nodded. "Of course. If you need to go now…"

He cut her off and shook his head sharply. "She's asleep and probably has been for hours, but I don't like her waking up alone. Sometimes she has bad coughing fits. She has a nebulizer, but she might need help if it gets bad, so I like to be there."

He said this matter-of-factly, but she sensed the pain underneath his words. It was strange to have just been so intimate with him and yet still be getting to know him.

"Okay." She pondered what else to say— that she was sorry he had to see his mother sick and face her mortality. But she sensed now wasn't the time. His chest rose and fell with a deep breath. In seconds, his breathing evened out. She lay beside him, her legs tangled with his and his chest warm under her palm. An immense relief lay within her. She'd finally ditched her virginity. Now, a different anxiety threaded through her. Noah wasn't just a fling. The moment in the woods today had made that clear, and he'd hammered the point home tonight. The cat in her nearly purred at the thought, but the rational, human side of her wasn't sure how to make sense of it. Her body was drained and sleep stole over her.

She woke hours later when Noah's lips met hers in the dark. She opened her eyes to find him standing by the bed dressed and ready to go. "Gotta go," he whispered into the quiet night.

"Hmm, 'kay."

Another kiss and he left, his footfall muted. She felt the rush of cool air drift in when he opened and closed the door.

7
_____

Noah woke to the sound of his mother coughing, a sound that had become painfully familiar. It tore him up inside every time because it reminded him she was sick and might not get better. He started to kick the covers off, but then he heard a pause and the distinct sound of her nebulizer humming. The coughing stopped. He lay still in the bed. His mother tended to get frustrated if he hovered too much, so when it seemed like she had things in hand, he tried to give her space. The wispy winter light of dawn was visible outside his window. He'd forgotten to close the curtains when he got home early this morning. He rolled his head to the side and stared out.

The sun's rays were reaching up into the sky above the trees. Balsam firs were dusted with fresh snow that had fallen during the night. A cardinal flew to the feeder behind the house, a cheery red spark in the white landscape.

Lily—her mountain lion, so lithe and sensual—sauntered into his thoughts. A primal tug stirred within him. Just thinking about last night, and his body came to life. He couldn't quite wrap his brain around the fact that she'd been a virgin. The way she was—wild, abandoned—nearly brought him to his knees. If he hadn't seen her yesterday in the woods, his mountain lion in full charge, he might have had second thoughts with her last night when she'd told him she was a virgin. He had a flicker of doubt, but then she'd gone and wrapped her hands around his cock. Her bright blue eyes looking up at him through her lashes shredded any resistance. He kicked the covers back again and strode to the shower. Rock hard with Lily nowhere near was not the time to lounge in bed.

A few hours later, he kicked the snow off his boots when he stepped through the door at Roxanne's Country Store. The scent of fresh baked bread and coffee led him straight to the deli in back. The hum of conversation filtered around him as he waited for Roxanne. She pushed through the swinging door into the back, a wide smile gracing her face the moment she saw him.

"Hey Noah! Coffee?" she asked, her blonde ponytail swinging in an arc when she turned at the sound of the oven buzzer. She quickly rotated some loaves of bread in the oven and returned her attention to him.

"It's always coffee," he replied sardonically.

Roxanne chuckled as she quickly grabbed a mug and filled it for him. "Habit. I ask even if I almost always know the answer." She paused, her eyes narrowing. "Did you happen to be leaving The Trailhead last night with Lily North?"

Noah took a sip of coffee and leaned his hip against the counter. Catamount was small enough that it was hard to keep anything quiet. He wished he knew how Lily felt about it because the whole world could know they were together as far as he was concerned. But the depth of his feelings when it came to his shifter self and the reality of life weren't always aligned. He knew she was meant to be his, but he wasn't quite so sure how they'd go from last night's earth-shattering intimacy to a commitment. Not to mention, he wasn't exactly experienced with relationships of the romantic kind—at all. While his lion side would have roared the news, his human side held glimmers of doubt and uncertainty. Human emotions tended to be weighted with complications—whether they made sense or not.

He met Roxanne's eyes, kind with a glint of humor, and shrugged. "Maybe."

Roxanne put her hands on her hips and glared at him. "Don't maybe me. Lily is one of my best friends. I'm not asking to be gossipy. Gail Anderson told me she saw you walking with Lily in the parking lot there. If Gail is wondering what's up, you can bet everyone else will start wondering soon. Gossip is like brushfire here—you can't stop it. Back to my point, I'm kind of protective of Lily, so you'd better be honest with me."

Noah took another fortifying sip of coffee. He respected Roxanne, so hearing about her protectiveness of Lily gave him pause. "Okay, yes. We had dinner there." He considered what else to say. To say he was sailing in uncharted waters with Lily didn't even come close to capturing how off kilter he felt. The morning he'd driven to town to meet his mother for her chemo appointment, his mind and heart had been firmly fixed where they'd been for years. Romance and commitment of any kind was not for him. His parents' marriage had left nothing but distaste for the mere concept. Then, he'd stopped to help Lily with her tire. The wheels starting spinning and lust took over. He'd thought even yesterday he could get things under control. It wasn't as if he'd never had casual dalliances, but they'd always been just that—with no risk of anything more. When he'd been roaming through the forest yesterday afternoon and seen Lily through the trees, his world tilted and spun sideways. He couldn't consider anything other than her being his...completely. Now, he had to figure out how to make sense of that. In the sharp, cold light of a wintry day, he wondered if he was half crazy.

Roxanne must have noticed something in his expression. Her eyes softened. "Ahh, so that's how it is."

Noah shifted his weight and took yet another gulp of coffee. At this rate, he'd need another cup of coffee in record time. "What do you mean?"

"I mean you look like you were whacked over the head. Lily's pretty amazing. She has a heart of gold and deserves a good guy like you. As long as you keep your head out of your ass and don't do anything stupid. Especially if you're thinking you're just going to fool around with her." Roxanne's tone held an edge of warning.

He shook his head. "No worries there. Just trying to figure out how the hell to deal with this. I wasn't..." He paused and cleared his throat. "...expecting Lily. Honestly, maybe you could give me some advice."

Roxanne smiled ruefully. "Just be good to Lily. If you're not, I'll kick your ass. So will her brother."

Noah nodded. "Right then. How about another cup of coffee?" He held up his empty mug.

After Roxanne refilled his coffee, he snagged a table and perused the newspaper for a few minutes. When he drove home shortly thereafter, he noticed a gray pickup truck following him. He slowed down enough to identify Kirk Hogan in the driver's seat. His phone rang, interrupting the radio.

When he answered, Jake North's voice came over the speakers in his truck. He experienced a flash of relief. He wasn't afraid of Kirk, but he'd like someone to be aware Kirk was following him.

"Noah, it's Jake."

"Hey there. Glad you called. Kirk Hogan appears to be following me home."

Noah heard a loud shuffle and then Jake's voice again. "I'm leaving the office now. I'll head up there. Did you see him somewhere?"

"Nope. Left Roxanne's a few minutes ago and he turned up behind me. No need for you to follow. I can handle him."

A door slammed in the background. "I'm sure you can, but it can't hurt to have a little backup. Remind me where your mom's house is."

After Noah gave him directions, Jake hung up. Noah didn't consider not going home because Kirk knew where his mother lived. He was plenty pissed, but he'd rather face Kirk's machinations head on. Moments later, he turned into the driveway. Kirk boldly drove in behind him and parked to the side.

Noah got out of his truck and walked over the Kirk. Kirk leaned against his truck when he stepped out. Kirk's eyes were muddy brown and insolent. His brown hair was messy. He stood a few inches shorter than Noah. When Noah approached him, Kirk's stare weakened. Noah felt he was looking at a man who'd taken a few too many wrong turns in life and was scrambling to find power however he could.

Noah came to a stop a few feet in front of Kirk and waited. Kirk bold façade flickered in the silence. The sound of tires on gravel announced Jake's arrival. Jake came to an abrupt stop behind Kirk's truck, effectively blocking him.

"So Kirk, what the hell is going on?" Jake said, his voice threaded with anger, as he strode quickly to them.

Kirk looked between Noah and Jake and rolled his eyes. "You guys think you're so fuckin' badass. Busy trying to protect Catamount shifters. Who gives a shit? Some of us don't want to keep protecting our legacy and bullshit. I'd like to make some good money off my skills, and I'm not alone. Why don't you two back the fuck off and leave it be? Who put you onto me anyway?"

Noah glanced at Jake and back to Kirk. "Maybe some shifters don't give a shit, but this smuggling network's already getting way too much attention from law enforcement. The wrong people find out and you'll wish for the time when shifters were just a myth. Ever thought about what it could mean if the government finds out who we are and what we can do? We could be monitored, tracked, controlled and more. Take my word for it. I was in the Special Forces for years. I'm far more aware than I'd like to be of what the government is willing to do if they feel there's a threat. Shifters don't need to be made into one."

Kirk smirked and looked to Jake. "Just because you're all high and mighty with Dane and Hank and your founding families bullshit doesn't mean you have all the power."

Noah glanced at Jake and knew he understood where his mind was going. They'd already been wondering about Callen's family. There were four founding families of shifters. Lily and Jake's family, the North's; Dane and Shana's family, the Ashworth's; Roxanne's family, the Morgan's; and Callen's family, the Peyton's. Of those four, the Peyton's had long been the most vocal about using shifter powers. Callen's death had opened a chasm within the shifter community with those shifters who were close to the

Peyton's closing ranks and proclaiming there was no way any other family members could be involved. Then, Randall had been arrested for kidnapping Dane's fiancée. Now, Brad, the last brother alive and not in jail, was linked to Kirk.

The final question remained as to whether Wallace Peyton, the father of them all, was involved. Wallace was a political animal. He'd been mayor of Catamount for many years some time ago. He ran the family's logging business and held tight to the massive fortune earned by his ancestors in the heyday of the timber industry. Wallace would not appreciate Kirk's boasting. He liked to pull the strings. He'd been laying low since Callen's death and Randall's arrest, insisting shifters needed to understand Callen had gone rogue and persuaded his younger, gullible brother to go along with him.

Jake shrugged in reply to Kirk's comment. "Is this your way of telling us Wallace Peyton's running the show on this end of the smuggling network?" He went straight past Kirk's insinuations.

Kirk's eyes widened. While he might want to create the impression he could throw his weight around, he knew perfectly well

Wallace wouldn't want anyone to think he was linked to this. He shook his head. "No," he sputtered. "I'm just saying not everyone thinks all the secrecy's been a good idea. We have ways to use our powers to make some serious cash. We're not hurting anyone. Drugs are gonna be sold and smuggled whether shifters are involved or not." His eyes narrowed again as he glanced between Noah and Jake. "You saw what happened to Chloe. If you want to put your family at risk, don't go blaming me if they come after you." His eyes slid toward the house where Noah's mother stood in the window.

Anger flashed through Noah. He was done. He took one swift stride, his hand locking around Kirk's throat and lifting him in the air. He shoved Kirk against the truck, easing his grip just enough for Kirk to breathe. "Do not fuck with my family. Do you understand? You forget I'm not all wrapped up in shifter honor and bullshit like that. My family might be the dregs in this town, but I know damn well most of the shifters around here want nothing to do with your garbage. If you keep threatening people, I will make you regret it."

Kirk kicked his feet out and tried to tear

Noah's hand away. Noah held firm, pushing his elbow against Kirk's chest. He eased his grip and allowed Kirk to slide down to the ground. Kirk slumped against the side of the truck, his eyes wary as he stared at Noah. Jake had remained silent. When Noah glanced his way, he saw barely leashed fury flash in Jake's eyes, but he held still, watching and waiting. As they stood there in the icy air, another car drove past the house. Noah immediately recognized it. Wallace Peyton was the only one in town who drove a fully decked out Cadillac, an entirely impractical car in Maine.

Kirk's eyes bounced from the car slowly easing by, to Jake and then Noah. He swore abruptly and shifted, bounding off into the woods. Jake didn't hesitate and shifted as well, leaping to a run. Noah met his mother's eyes through the window. She nodded in the direction of Kirk. Noah shifted and raced after Kirk and Jake.

Noah caught up to Jake quickly. Jake appeared to be measuring his speed, maintaining a set distance from Kirk. Noah matched his speed. Kirk wove through the trees, the black tip of his tail flicking. Snow kicked up around them as they bounded through the woods. Noah's fur rippled in the wind gusting through the forest. They saw Kirk weave and turn out of sight. Noah bolted ahead to catch a glimpse of Kirk cutting along the edge of an abandoned quarry. He was in clear view once he crested a small rise though he appeared to think he'd lost them as he slowed down.

After another few minutes, the forest thinned and they approached the back end of Wallace Peyton's property. Noah and Jake came to a stop where they were shielded by the trees. Kirk approached a barn and shifted back into human form before slipping inside the barn. Jake tossed his head, gesturing toward the forest. In silence, they retraced their brief sprint.

$\sim$

A WHILE LATER, Noah leaned against the counter in his mother's kitchen. Carol had insisted on offering coffee to Jake who lounged at the kitchen table, graciously talking with her.

His mother glanced between him and Jake. "I'd have bet Wallace Peyton was behind all of this," she said bluntly.

Noah eyed her and took a swallow of coffee before addressing Jake. "My mom keeps a low profile, but she usually knows a lot more than she lets on." He swung to his mother. "Mind filling us in?"

Carol smiled softly. "Oh, I don't have any special information, but I went to school with Wallace. He always wanted to be the big guy. I never quite thought being mayor and inheriting money would satisfy him. He's always been sneaky and liked to get away with things. He was also known to make comments about how shifters could have had so much more if they weren't afraid to go public. When Callen was in high school with you, he was the same way. That's all I'm saying. Wallace probably couldn't resist this when he found out about it."

Jake eyed her thoughtfully. "Funny, but most everyone is afraid to say much about Wallace."

Carol shrugged. "It's easier when you don't have much to lose," she said. "I don't have to worry about him talking trash about me. I already spent too long married to the biggest jerk in town. Wallace doesn't even notice me."

"Mom..." Noah started to interject, but she waved him off.

"Oh honey, don't worry about me. I'm a realist. I'm as happy as I can be these days. You're home and my life is peaceful. Whatever you do, be careful going after Wallace."

Noah stepped to his mother's side where she sat at the table and gave her quick hug. He swallowed against the tightness in his throat. He didn't need Jake seeing him fall apart.

When he stepped back to lean on the counter, Jake appeared unruffled. He met Noah's eyes. "Your mom's smarter than we've been. I only recently started to consider Wallace could be involved. I guess I didn't think he'd want to dirty his hands."

Carol shook her head. "He wouldn't want anyone to know it, but the Wallace I knew would love to think he was getting away with something, especially if it involved money."

8

———

Lily leaned her head back on the couch and stared at the ceiling, which happened to be finished with wood that had a mesmerizing scatter of knots in it. She could stare at it for hours, aimlessly counting the knots while she vainly attempted to get her mind off of Noah. Even trying to think of something else sent her thoughts cartwheeling into the memory of the other night. The way his hands felt on her skin, his lips on her body and the feel of him inside of her—her body flushed at the memory.

"Dammit!" She stood up abruptly and began pointlessly tidying the living room.

Noah had called her yesterday, and she

had let his call go to voice mail. She couldn't quite figure out how to face him. She was so stirred up by what happened, she didn't know what to do. All those years of trying to ditch her virginity and she finally had. Now, she was so worked up over her feelings about Noah, she was mired in anxiety. Seeing as her experience with men was decidedly limited, she couldn't say she knew what to expect, but she didn't think it was typical to be so utterly in thrall with someone that it bordered on ridiculous. She couldn't imagine what Noah thought. The cat in her knew what lay between them couldn't be casual, but the cold light of day made it hard to remember.

Noah had left two messages yesterday and another this morning. She still hadn't gathered the courage to call him back. That itself was making her feel silly. There was a sudden sharp knock at her door. It was evening, but already dark since they were deep into winter now. She walked to the door. When she opened it, Noah stood there, his hand raised as if to knock again. The moment she saw him, it was as if a switch was flipped inside. Heat suffused through her and her belly clenched.

His amber eyes coasted over her face. He held still, as if he was holding himself back. "Can I come in?"

She nodded and stepped back from the door. A gust of icy air blew in with him and swirled with loose flakes of snow when she closed the door. She walked over to the kitchen counter, needing something to lean against, to hold her up.

He followed her and stood before her, his dark hair tousled. He didn't look away, his gaze holding her. Her pulse quickened. She tried to think of what to say.

His voice broke through the quiet. "Did I misunderstand something the other night?"

His eyes held a glimmer of uncertainty and confusion.

While she'd be the first to acknowledge she had no idea how to handle her feelings, she suddenly felt badly for avoiding his calls.

"No! I just...well..." She flushed deeply but forced herself to keep talking. "This is all new to me, if that wasn't obvious. When you called yesterday, I wasn't sure what to say because I don't know you all that well yet, and I don't really know what you want and..." Her words were flying out so fast, she had to pause and gulp in air.

Noah's eyes softened slightly. His shoulders rose and fell with his own deep breath. "It might not seem all new to me, but it is in a way. Maybe we don't know each other that well in the usual way. All I know is I don't really care because I *know* you the way I need to." His words were rough and raw.

His words cracked through the confusion in her mind. The knot of anxiety in her chest tightened and let loose at once, a flash of joy racing through her. Her heart clenched. Desire unfurled inside her. The air around them felt alive, shimmering in the intensity. His presence left her struggling to catch her breath. Heat spread through her limbs like wildfire.

Lost in sensation and unable to put words to her feelings, she communicated the only way she knew how. She stepped closer to him. He carried the scent of snow and wood smoke. His jacket hung open, and she placed her palms on his chest, sliding them up, one pausing over the beat of his heart, before pushing his jacket off his shoulders and leaning up to kiss him. He didn't hesitate, his mouth came against hers—open and hot. He kissed her fiercely, hungrily. She felt the tug of him from inside out and dove into the flames that swirled within and around them.

Noah's strong arms came around her, lifting her with ease. He settled her on the counter and slid his palms up her thighs, firmly pushing them apart as he stepped between them. The heat of his palms filtered through the denim encasing her legs. Wet heat pooled between her thighs. Her pulse skittered beyond control, her breath became ragged. His palms kept moving, curling around the edges of her hips, the soft flesh giving under the pressure. Goose bumps prickled on the surface of her skin when his hands slid under the soft cotton of her shirt, coasting up her sides, his thumbs flicking her nipples through the lace of her bra. He didn't pause as his hands pushed her shirt up, the fabric bunching until he lifted it up and over her head. With a flick, it fell in a rumple on the kitchen floor.

Desire pounded through her. All he'd done was take her shirt off, and she was near out of her mind. She glanced up to find his eyes on hers, waiting. Without a word, he slipped his thumb under the clasp between her breasts and snapped it open. Her breasts tumbled free—hot, heavy and aching for his touch. He stepped back, and she felt bereft at the absence. A small whimper fell from her lips. He abruptly tugged his shirt off. It joined hers on the floor before he stepped back between her legs. His hands cupped her bottom and pulled her close. The feel of his hard, heated length against the moist heat between her thighs sent a sharp spike of pleasure spinning through her.

"Needed to feel your skin," he said, his voice low and taut, as his hands coasted up her back.

She arched, like the cat she was, into his touch, gasping at the feel of his hard muscles against her breasts. Need swept through her, its force overwhelming. She couldn't get close enough fast enough. Noah's lips met hers again in a hot, wet kiss. Her hands roamed over his body, her legs curled around his hips as she strained against him. After years and years of wondering what she might be missing, she suddenly couldn't be without it. Her channel throbbed, desperate for the feel of him inside of her again. He tore his mouth from hers, lips, tongue and teeth tracing down her neck to her breasts. He teased her first with soft nips, circling her nipples with his tongue, before he finally took one and then the other in his mouth. She cried out at the sharp, sweet pain when he bit down. Pressure gathered, spinning her tighter and tighter inside.

She stroked her hand along his hard length, savoring his groan when she unbuttoned his fly and slipped her hand inside. She shimmied out of his arms and slipped off the counter before he had a chance to stop her. Though she'd only been with him once, she sensed he was accustomed to being in control, to directing the action. He started to step away, but she grabbed his hips. "No! I want to do this." *This* being to find out what it felt like to taste his cock.

She moved too fast for him to stop her, kneeling before him and shoving his jeans down far enough to free him. Anticipation and anxiety thrummed through her. Her limited experience brought a slight pause, but she swatted it away. When she stroked up and down his length, he groaned, his head falling back.

"Lily, you don't need to..."

She ignored him and swiftly stroked her tongue along the underside of his cock before taking him in her mouth. She explored the length of him, stroking up and down as deeply as she could. She tasted the subtle salty tang of his pre-cum. He pulsed inside of her and suddenly stepped back, lifting her smoothly. His strength was such he held her with one arm and tore at her jeans with the other. She kicked them off once they were loose.

The granite of the kitchen counter was cool on her bottom. His eyes met hers. The sight of his arousal, so blatant, made her channel throb with need. Held within his amber gaze, a hot shiver raced through her when he slid a finger into her folds and commenced to notch her higher and higher. He stroked inside, his fingers sliding in and out, his thumb coasting across her clit, the touch just enough to drive her wild, but not enough to give her release. Everything narrowed to sensation, to the feel of Noah's hard body, his fingers driving her wilder and wilder, tightening the screws of desire until she was writhing and pleading. Only then did he lean down and bring his mouth against her, swiftly sucking her clit inside, his tongue swirling around it. Her climax came in a noisy burst as she shuddered against his mouth.

Anchored only by the feel of one of his

hands curled around her hip, she opened her eyes. He fumbled in his pocket, his jeans low on his hips. The sight of his cock and knowing what it felt like to have him inside her made her ache. He rolled a condom on, his eyes never leaving hers. He stepped between her thighs and curled his hands under her bottom, bringing her to the edge of the counter. He nudged into her folds. She gasped at the sensation. Yet again, he didn't rush though she was near desperate for him. Holding her hips close with one hand, he used the other to drag the head of his cock back and forth through her folds—so sensitized from her orgasm that pleasure echoed and built again—until she was mad with need.

"Noah...please..."

"Yes..." he whispered, his voice almost reverent, as he surged inside of her.

She sensed he was trying to hold back, to be gentle. She didn't want gentle. She shimmied closer, plastering herself to him, glorying in the feel of his muscled body against her, and curled her legs around his hips. She tugged him closer, sliding her hands up his back and down, her nails scoring him. He growled, his mouth at her ear, the gust of his breath sending a hot shiver through her. His strokes deepened, his hips drummed into her. The ache inside was eased by the flex and stretch of him within her, the push and pull. His muscles were tight under her touch, power vibrating from him with every stroke. He slipped a hand where they were joined, his thumb circling her clit. Once and then twice, and she cried out, as another orgasm crashed over her, rippling through her in waves.

Noah's head fell into her shoulder and then flew back as he thrust a final time. She felt the pulse of him inside as he shuddered against her. The sound of their broken breathing surrounded them. She nestled into his embrace, listening to the beat of his heart against her ear.

This—this space where her mind didn't try to crowd out what her senses and her soul knew—was where she felt more at home, more at peace than she'd ever been. She didn't know how much time passed. Noah lifted his head. Cool air slipped into the spaces between them, and she shivered.

～

NOAH STOOD at the counter in Roxanne's Country Store and waited while Roxanne poured a cup of coffee for him. She turned back to him, immediately sliding a hot cup of coffee across the counter. Tucking a pen in her hair, she put a hand on her hip and arched a brow.

"What?" he finally asked.

"Ran into your mom this morning. I was up at the hospital taking my mom for some routine tests, and she was in the waiting room. She thinks you're in love with Lily. Were you planning to mention anything else about Lily to me?" Her blue eyes held a challenging glint.

Noah flushed and shifted on his feet. "Damn, what's this with the third degree? Must have missed the memo where I need to report back to you." He was annoyed at the questions because he was used to keeping his private life private.

Roxanne glared at him. "You don't have to report back to me, but maybe you could clue me in. I told you, she's one of my best friends. If your mom's right, then I'm thrilled." She paused and the glare left her eyes, worry replacing it. "Look, I already told you I'm kind of protective of Lily. She's a pretty private person, and she doesn't do things lightly. Her family can be an oversized presence around here, so she gets lost in the shuffle. I don't mean to seem nosy, but I don't want to see her hurt. I don't think you'd set out to hurt her..."

Noah realized he was annoyed with Roxanne for trying to protect Lily from him when he'd never even think of hurting Lily. He cut her off. "You don't need to worry. My mom's right about Lily. I love her." His heart sped as he said the words aloud and wondered if he'd completely lost his mind. In the span of weeks, the pendulum in his heart had swung wildly in the direction of Lily. Irrational though it may seem, he knew he loved her. He considered Lily's words last night when she commented she didn't know him that well. What he knew of her relied more on the ephemeral, primal instincts of his lion—and he didn't doubt those instincts for a second. Yet, he had only the broad strokes of her life beyond that. Her family held a position of power and prestige in Catamount. They were one of the founding families of shifters, but they didn't throw their weight around like the Peyton's did, thus garnering more respect and goodwill as a result.

Roxanne's comment made him realize why he may have overlooked Lily before. Her parents and Jake were in the thick of the social world of Catamount, while Lily was quieter and more introspective. He thought back to the day he'd given her a ride into town. She was so sexy and cute, she set his body afire. But he hadn't really noticed her before. His encounters with her when they were growing up had been mostly from a distance, so her tendency to withdraw would have kept her off his radar. He was so focused on avoiding his father's wrath, worrying about his mother, and generally trying to make no waves that his attention was scattered anyway.

Roxanne cleared her throat. "Yoo hoo. Anyone home?"

Noah glanced up to find her warm blue eyes on him. He shrugged.

"You zoned out right after you said you loved Lily, so you didn't even give me a chance..." She paused and leaned across the counter, cupping his face in her hands. "...to do this." She gave him a smacking kiss on the cheek and leaned back, her smile wide.

Noah was so startled he spilled his coffee. Roxanne didn't miss a beat and immediately wiped the counter and refilled his cup.

Her eyes sobered as she slid the fresh cup of coffee across the counter to him. "So, what's Lily got to say about you two?"

"Good question. This kinda came out of the blue. I haven't exactly had much experience with relationships."

Roxanne smiled softly and shrugged. "Lily's pretty straightforward. Maybe you should just tell her how you feel."

He rolled his eyes. "You make it sound so easy."

Roxanne nudged her chin up. "Well, maybe you should ask her brother about it."

Noah swore and turned to look over his shoulder. Jake strode into the deli area of the store, aiming straight for Noah. Noah was nowhere near wanting to discuss his feelings about Lily with Jake. He could only guess at it, but he imagined Jake was on the high end of the scale when it came to protecting his sister.

Jake came to a stop at his side. He nodded at Roxanne and turned to Noah. "Saw your truck outside. Thought you might want to know it looks like your mom's hunch about Wallace was right. Between Hank and I, we managed to dig up the digital trail for him. He's in as deep as Callen was. Hank's working with the DA to draw up an arrest warrant for him. I thought maybe we could stop by Derek Miller's place and see if he's heard anymore from Kirk. It's a loose end I'd like to tie up while we wait."

Roxanne's eyes darted between them. "Holy shit. Should've known Wallace was behind this. He's always been a tad too high and mighty for me, but he loves money and power." She looked to Jake. "Any idea on how long it'll take to get him behind bars?"

Jake shrugged. "As long as it takes Hank and the DA to feel confident they have a solid case. Wallace will fight like hell, so they want to be sure."

Noah nodded. "If you wanna head out to Derek's place, anytime works for me."

Jake nodded sharply. "Let me get a coffee, and then let's go."

9

———

"But Dad, you promised I could go to the movies tonight!" Jasmine Miller exclaimed before stomping out of her father's office. She left the door open behind her, brisk winter air gusting inside.

Derek rolled his eyes and strode to the door. "The deal was homework done first. You still have plenty of time," he called out before swinging the door shut.

Noah and Jake stood inside Derek's office at the main quarry. Jasmine could be seen striding to another building and slamming inside.

Derek chuckled. "She'll get the homework done." He shook his head. "I thought I'd be an expert at the whole teen thing.

Man, it's way worse when it's your daughter." He ran a hand through his hair and stepped back to his desk, sitting down in the chair and gesturing to the chairs on the other side. "What's up guys? I have a pretty obvious guess with what's been going down lately, but fill me in."

After a quick summary, Derek's eyes widened at the mention of Wallace. "Hot damn. Kirk bragged about being in with some heavies around Catamount. With Callen and Randall's involvement and seeing Kirk with Brad, I shoulda guessed. So what now?"

"We wait for the police and the DA's office to do the legwork on a solid case. Meanwhile, we wanted to see if you'd heard anything else from Kirk," Jake replied.

Derek nodded. "The usual. He keeps asking about the damn quarry, but since it was reported to the police, we haven't seen Brad's truck out there anymore." He sighed. "Kirk's desperate. He can't hold a job, he's using too much of I don't even know what. Far as I can tell, he thinks this smuggling thing is easy money and no risk as long as they can convince everyone else to ignore it."

As Noah and Jake walked outside a while

later, Kirk pulled up. Derek had followed them outside, intending to head over to check on the status of Jasmine's homework. He paused beside them instead. Kirk leapt out of his truck, slamming the door. He strode to Derek and leaned right into his face.

"You just couldn't keep your damn mouth shut? All you had to do was let us use the old quarry sometimes. Now I've got Brad calling me telling me the deal is off. I'm losing serious money here!" Kirk swung away, his eyes bouncing to Noah and Jake.

"Fuck you." He spit his words out.

Derek's eyes looked past him at another truck turning into the gravel drive to the quarry. "What the hell is Brad doing out here again?" he asked, his eyes swinging back to Kirk.

Kirk sneered. "He's fuckin' pissed, that's what."

Brad Peyton skidded to a stop and slammed out of his truck. As he strode toward them, he shifted, leaping forward with a roar. In seconds, Noah, Jake and Kirk shifted. Derek didn't. He shook his head firmly and stepped back. Kirk swiped at him, but backed down when Jake snarled and stepped between them. Noah flexed into his lion, his fur rippling in the cold winter air. He circled back away from the cluster. He sensed Brad's only intention was to intimidate, but he watched and waited. Jake growled at Kirk, bodily shoving him away from Derek. Brad swiped at Jake, but Jake dodged quickly. In a flash, Brad bolted with Kirk following. Jake and Noah bounded behind them. Jake's lion met Noah's eyes. Again, communication was seamless between them. They'd hang back to see where Brad and Kirk were trying to lead them and assess their options then.

Noah savored the feel of his lion. Strength and power surged in waves of heat. Snow flew up around them as they crossed the field behind the quarry and dashed into the woods. Brad was headed toward his father's property. Another glance with Jake, and they kept holding back. This time, they followed the path onto Wallace's property. A clearing opened, and another mountain lion stood on a small rise. The lion couldn't be anyone other than Wallace. Noah couldn't recall if he'd ever seen Wallace in lion form, but this lion was tall, regal and aged. Another glance with Jake, and they lunged forward, swiftly catching up to Brad and Kirk. Noah didn't hesitate. With a roar, he leapt on Brad's back, sinking his claws in and tossing him to the ground. Whatever Wallace wanted, he would have to negotiate with his son on the edge of danger.

Brad lashed out, catching Noah in the shoulder. Kirk turned and attempted to join the tussle, but Jake dashed in front of him and engaged him in a fight. Claws and fur flew. Growls and snarls dominated until Noah had Brad firmly pinned under his paw. Noah had sustained multiple scratches, but Brad never succeeded in escaping from Noah's grip. Noah held his throat in his teeth and snarled. Kirk had given up the fight much more quickly. Jake stood above him, his breath bellowing in the icy winter air.

The bite of iron seeped into Noah's mouth as he held firm on Brad's throat. Wallace shifted in the distance. He casually stood in his human form and stretched before gathering clothing dropped on the ground around him and walking over. When he reached them, his eyes traveled over them all. Noah and Jake exchanged another glance. In silent agreement, they didn't shift back into human form.

Wallace's eyes landed on Brad, his anger evident. "I should have known better than to involve you in this. You're too impulsive, too pushy." Wallace's gaze traveled to Jake and Noah. His lips curled in a sneer. "Wouldn't have guessed you'd be on their side," he commented, gesturing to Noah. "Your father was nothing more than a thief and a wife beater." Noah ignored Wallace and fought against the urge to claw at him. Mountain lions fought among each other, but within the shifter community, it was unheard of for a shifter to attack a human, even if the human in question was a shifter in their human form.

Wallace nodded to his son. "You can let him go. He won't be bothering you again."

Noah slowly released his hold. Brad remained in lion form, his breath labored. Blood streaked his fur. He ignored his father. Wallace remained silent as Jake released Kirk. Noah and Jake quietly padded away. The waited at a distance and watched as Wallace kicked at Brad until he shifted. Kirk followed. Noah and Jake continued their slow pace into the trees as Wallace's shouting carried across the distance.

"You stupid idiot! I told you asking

anyone about using their property for deliveries was stupid. You don't ask. You do what you want."

His voice faded as they moved deeper into the forest.

LILY STOOD IN THE SHOWER, savoring the steaming hot water raining down over her. She'd spent the afternoon stacking her woodpile. Snow started to fall, leaving her damp and chilled through by the time she was done. She'd been trying to keep busy, to keep her mind off of Noah. In such a short time, her thoughts about him had worn a groove in her mind. He danced along the edge of her consciousness almost all the time. Her body hummed in anticipation. She felt a hunger for him, it tugged at her, leaving her muddled and at whim to her body. The cat side of her relished the feeling while her human side was torn. She wanted to regain some semblance of control over herself. Just now, she craved his touch. Without thinking, she slipped her hand down into her curls and dipped into the slick moisture of her folds. Her touch was an echo of his. Her channel throbbed at the memory of his fingers inside her, playing her like an instrument. She didn't recognize the woman Noah elicited—wanton, heedless, and wild.

Her heart raced. Toying with herself, she blushed at the thought of his eyes on her. The intimacy between them seared through her, almost frightening her with its intensity. She dipped her finger into her channel, stroking into its soft clench. She couldn't help the gasp that escaped from her. Noah filled her mind while she teased herself. Soaked with want, she craved more. It wasn't enough, her touch only made her want Noah —his hard body, the feel of him filling her, stretching her. A whimper fell from her lips. She jumped at the sound of a soft knock.

"Lily?"

Her heart stuttered and sped at the sound of Noah's voice.

"Um, I'm in the shower."

Oh my god, oh my god, oh my god! Even though her body was ecstatic at his presence, she was mortified he'd almost caught her like this.

His soft chuckle made her smile. "Mind if I join you?"

Her body all but screamed for joy. "No, not at all."

Understatement of the century. She was fingering herself, desperate for Noah to be here with her, and now he was. *You are out of your mind and getting in way over your head.*

The shower door opened and Noah stepped inside. Her eyes landed on the long deep scratches scoring his chest and arms. She forgot her desire. Her throat tightened with fear.

"Noah! What happened?"

He stepped into the cascade of water first, closing his eyes and leaning his head back with a sigh. He ran his hands through his hair before tipping his head back up and meeting her eyes. In the misty light created by the steam, it felt as if they were in a co-coon. He reached for her, sliding his arms around her and pulling her close. Her body relaxed into his touch while her mind gnawed with worry.

She leaned her head up. "Don't try to distract me. Why are you all scratched up? I know what I'm seeing. You had a fight with someone, and I want to know who and why."

His eyes opened, that amber gaze igniting sparks in her belly. "I'm fine. Jake and I went out to Derek Miller's place to follow up. Long story short, Kirk and Brad showed up. Took us on a merry chase through the woods to Wallace's place. I'm not too sure what they meant to do, but I pinned Brad while Jake took care of Kirk."

Questions tumbled through her mind, but Noah's touch was distracting her beyond belief. One hand roamed on her bottom, the other sliding over the curve of her breast to toy with a nipple. Her breath hitched. He made her crazy. She was scared for him, and here she was already forgetting that, her body arching into him, wild with need. He was like a drug, one she couldn't live without. She forced herself to focus and looked up at him. What she saw in his eyes took her breath away. Molten heat swirled inside. Her heart battered against her ribcage. His gaze reached in and grabbed her heart. She stroked a hand up his chest, tracing the line of one of the scratches.

"I don't like seeing you like this," she whispered, her throat tight.

Water rolled down his skin. He lifted his hand and traced her mouth with his thumb. Her pulse raced out of control. Her belly clenched, lust piercing through her. In a swift motion, his lips replaced his thumb. His kisses just ruined her, wiped all thought from her mind. The only drive was to get closer, to meld her entire being with his. Their tongues tangled, their breath became one. She ran her hands up his chest, gasping when he tore his mouth from hers, his teeth nipping at her earlobe. His body was all muscle and strength. The feel of him only notched the ache inside her higher.

Noah rocked his hips into the cradle of hers, his arousal nudging her. Her sex clenched. His hands roamed over her, his touch rough. He blazed a trail down her neck with his lips and teeth, hot shivers racing behind. She curled her hand around his cock, glorying in the wet slide of her grip. A groan escaped him, his mouth latched onto a nipple, sucking and biting until she writhed against him. She lost all focus, desperate only to have him inside her.

He suddenly stepped back and started to open the shower door. She grabbed at him. "Where...?"

"Condom," he bit out.

Lily shook her head. "It doesn't matter. I'm on the pill. You know I was a virgin before, so..."

She flushed, suddenly embarrassed. She was acting like this was so much more than it was. Biting her lip, she stared at his chest, her eyes snagging on a scratch that traveled from his shoulder to his lower ribcage. It was angry and red and made her heart clench. Her feelings for him were too much, too intense, too soon.

Noah let the door fall closed and stepped close to her again, his arms sliding around her. Even surrounded by steam, hot water raining upon her, the heat of his touch echoed in her body. She forced herself to meet his eyes.

"You don't have to, you know. I'd give just about anything to feel what's it's like to be inside you without anything between us. In case you're wondering, I'm clean as a whistle. I haven't been too busy in that area anyway." He paused, a flicker of uncertainty in his eyes. "I know this is pretty new for us, but, uh, it's not something light for me."

Steam curled around them as Lily looked up into his amber gaze. Her insecurity faded. Though he hadn't spelled it out, as she hadn't, his eyes told her that he felt *this* between them just as intensely as she did. A drop of water rolled into the corner of her mouth. She licked it away and nodded. "I'm sure."

His eyes held hers for another beat before his mouth crashed to hers again. Hot, wet heat surrounded her—within and all around. His hands cupped her breasts, plumping them high for him to feast on her nipples, the alternating soft touch of his wicked tongue with the sharp bite of his teeth driving her mad. Liquid shivers raced through her. She pushed back and sank to her knees, taking him into her mouth. His hands threaded into her wet hair as she stroked up and down, bringing him fully into her mouth again and again and again. Until he abruptly stepped back and tugged her up, turning her to face the wall. His palm slid down her spine, the calloused skin sending sparks in its path. He cupped her bottom in his hands, roughly pushing her thighs apart. Her channel throbbed with need. She pushed back into his touch.

He stroked his fingers into her folds, soaked with her desire. He toyed with her, stroking around her entrance and circling her clit, before finally plunging his fingers inside her. She ground into his touch, but it wasn't enough. Pleasure whipsawed through her, pushing her closer and closer to the edge. Only when she cried out and begged did he nudge his cock into her entrance, slowly sliding his fingers out. He held still for a long moment until she wiggled against him. In a swift surge, he filled her and began to pound into her. The tile was cool under her palms, the contrast heightening the heat twisting inside of her. Without his strong grip on her hips, she'd have fallen. Everything centered on the feel of him moving in and out of her—the push and pull, the pounding. She wanted him deeper and arched into each stroke. He slipped a hand around her hip, sliding over the curve of her belly and pressing against her clit. The brief touch set loose the pressure gathered within her. Her climax wrenched through her, the pleasure so acute, she sobbed.

Another thrust into her channel as it clenched around him, and a guttural cry tore from Noah's throat as he pulsed into her. She felt his lips against the back of her neck before his head fell into the dip of her shoulder. Their ragged breathing mingled with the sound of water falling. They remained like that for long moments before he slowly straightened and pulled out of her. His touch never left her, his hands holding her hips firmly as she gathered herself and turned. She fumbled for the soap and quickly soaped herself and him. As she passed over the scratches marring his chest, she looked up at him. He was watching her, his gaze inscrutable. A flutter passed through her center.

"Don't think just because you distracted me, I'll forget to ask more about what happened today."

The corner of his mouth lifted in a small smile. "I didn't think you'd forget." He snatched the soap from her and made quick work of cleaning up while she rinsed. "Before we talk, I'm starving," he said bluntly as she toweled off a few minutes later.

10

———————

Noah kicked the snow off his boots as he stepped through the door into Jake's office. Jake had called him earlier and asked if he'd stop by to talk with Hank and Dane.

Noah happened to be looking down when he stepped inside, so when he looked up and saw Lily, it startled him. Instantly, he felt that deep pull inside whenever he saw her. Which was incredibly inconvenient considering that her brother was right there in the room, alongside Dane Ashworth who happened to be good friends with the family, and Hank Anderson, Catamount's police chief.

Lily's blue eyes met his across the room.

His heart tightened and lust coiled in his veins. It was going to take all of his discipline to keep his feelings at bay. Shifters were tuned into each other. Male mountain lions were fiercely protective of their mates. The depth of feelings that came along with being a shifter wasn't particularly helpful if one wanted to mask their feelings with another shifter. It wasn't that Noah wanted to hide how he felt about Lily, but he knew her brother finding out about them needed to happen on her terms. He highly doubted she wanted that to be right now in front of a small audience. He took a deep breath and nodded to Dane and Hank before meeting Jake's eyes.

"Thanks for stopping by," Jake said, by way of greeting.

"No problem." Noah realized his tendency to be perfunctory was instantly magnified by how busy he was trying to keep his body under control. It took all he had not to look at Lily again. He glanced around the room. Dane was lounging on the edge of a file cabinet while Hank sat in one of the chairs by Jake's desk. Jake sat across from him, and Lily sat at another desk behind Jake. Noah wasn't sure if he should sit and was relieved when Jake gestured for him to do so.

"Need some coffee, or anything?" Jake asked.

Dane chuckled and caught Noah's eyes. "His coffee sucks, so unless you're desperate, I'd pass."

Lily giggled. Noah couldn't stop his eyes from slanting in her direction. Her hair fell in loose waves around her shoulders. She stopped giggling, her eyes landing on his. Her perfect bow mouth was bright, her lips soft and pink. Her cheeks were flushed. Her eyes tilted up, the feline hint of her was soft, giving her face a heart-shaped look. She was somehow sexy, cute, shy and bold all at once. He had to close his eyes because his mind went straight to how her lips felt underneath his. *Holy hell.* He could *not* get a hard on right now.

That's how helpless he felt when it came to Lily. She didn't quite seem to realize it, but he was putty in her hands. Whatever she wanted, he'd give it to her with no hesitation. He couldn't believe this is what it had come to. Before he stopped by the side of the road that winter morning, he had *no* plans of considering a relationship with anyone. He simply didn't think it was a good idea. He wouldn't have described himself as commitment phobic, or one of those guys more interested in playing the field. No, he hadn't believed in love, hadn't believed the knee-weakening passion he felt for Lily was even possible. When you don't even know something can exist, you have no way to prepare for it. Lily had blindsided him.

He mentally shook himself. *Dude, get it together. Fast. Her brother's sitting two feet away.* He took a breath and opened his eyes, purposefully keeping them trained on the desk. Conveniently, Jake and Dane were bantering about Jake's shitty coffee. No one seemed to have noticed he'd been preoccupied.

"It's a damn miracle you didn't starve yourself before you wised up about Phoebe. Count yourself lucky you love a woman who's one hell of a cook and makes amazing coffee," Dane commented with a grin.

Jake's return smile was unabashed. "Damn straight. That's not why I love her, but it's an awesome bonus."

Lily stood. Noah had to shackle his impulse to do so much more than briefly glance her way. "How about I run down to Rox-anne's and bring back some coffee?"

Jake readily agreed with Dane and Hank chiming in as well. Noah realized his silence must have gone on too long when Jake said his name.

Noah glanced to Jake, firmly keeping his eyes away from Lily. "Yeah?"

"Did you want some coffee from Rox-anne's?" Jake asked.

"Oh sure." That was about all he could manage, but then Lily had to go and ask what kind.

He turned her way. The soft flush on her cheeks had deepened. She stood by the corner of Jake's desk. Noah could feel her from where he sat and see the pulse flut-tering in her neck. He clenched his fists in his pockets. "Shot in the dark works for me."

Lily nodded. "Just one shot of espresso in the coffee?"

He managed to nod and blessedly could look away. She asked the rest for their prefer-ences. What should have been a boring topic sent his blood, hot and thick, surging through his veins. His mind relived the sound of her voice when she cried out last night in the shower and the feel of her channel clenching his cock. He had to close his eyes again. When he opened them, he counted the trees in view through the windows. Conversation continued around him as Lily pulled her jacket on and left.

Relief and disappointment warred within him. He was relieved she was gone, so he could pull himself together, and disappointed because he instantly missed her. Fortunately, Hank took over the reins of conversation, pulling Dane and Jake onto the topic of the investigation.

"Here's where we stand, guys. Randall's still tight-lipped. I thought he'd get bored being in jail by now because it's been awhile. But he hasn't had many visitors, even from his family, so I'm guessing he's not up to speed on what's going on outside. Only visitor's been his mother." Hank paused and glanced to Jake.

"Still nothing on her?" Hank asked.

Jake shook his head firmly. "Far as I can tell, she's clean. At least, from what I can gather with her online trail. She and Wallace divorced years ago. I was young enough I don't remember much about it, but I remember it was ugly."

Hank nodded. "Hell, it was awful. He

dragged her through the mud in court. Back to Wallace, looks like Callen's the one that originally stumbled on this smuggling network, but once he brought his dad in, Wallace took the lead. That stuff you found the other day on him was a goldmine. He's been in almost weekly communication with one of the guys out in Montana about deliveries. I'd like to keep waiting, but I think we have enough to arrest him. I'm afraid if we wait too long while he knows we're onto him, he'll have time to do some clean up."

The conversation continued with Hank laying out his plan around how to handle the arrest of Wallace, while he looked to Jake, Dane and Noah for planning on how to handle the fallout and manage some of the loose ends, such as Kirk.

Though Noah had been proud of his time in the military and was accustomed to working on investigations and stealth missions in the Special Forces, he'd always thought of that part of himself as entirely separate from Catamount. Here, he'd never been a decorated soldier. He'd been nothing more than the son of a man who was rough and dragged down everyone around him. His father's family had been one generation after another of violent men who toed the edge of criminal activity. He couldn't quite believe Jake, Dane and Hank had so easily accepted him into the ranks of shifters they turned to in situations like this. His throat tightened, but his heart eased. He didn't want to carry the burden of his father everywhere he went in Catamount.

He glanced between the men. "Hope I'm not covering old territory, but you guys have been working this one longer than me. Have we followed up on all the other loose ends? Are we thinking that if we can make the link to Wallace, that'll cut this off at the head in Catamount?"

Hank shrugged and shook his head sadly. "That's my hunch. The only loose end would be your uncle. Theo isn't talking either. He doesn't seem to have the position or resources to have much weight to this. I'd be curious to know your thoughts on him though. Do you think he was involved in the organization, or just doing grunt work for the cash?"

Noah considered his uncle. "Like you said, Theo doesn't have the resources or the planning capacity to be doing much. But he's always after easy money and doesn't care much how he gets it. I don't know if it'll be worth it, but I don't mind trying to talk to him. We were never close. He's my father's brother, and needless to say, I wasn't close to my father either. But maybe Theo will talk if I try."

LILY STOOD in line at Roxanne's Country Store and tapped her foot restlessly. She had to get out of Jake's office, but even now, after a brisk walk that left her ears almost numb from the cold, her body hummed with electricity. Jake asked her to come by today to help with a few things, but she had no idea Noah was stopping by. Jake would flip his lid if he knew she was with Noah. Well, it wasn't Noah specifically, but any guy. Somehow, and damned if she knew how, Jake knew she was a virgin. Or rather, used to be one. A few years ago, he'd warned her away from another shifter in Catamount who'd briefly shown interest in her. At the time, Jake insisted the guy was only after her family connections. She hadn't been interested enough to care, but in the midst of Jake's warning, he'd let slip that he didn't want her to lose her virginity to a jerk. Speechless, she'd merely turned a special shade of red and stammered her way out of the conversation. She suspected Phoebe had cued him in. Before he and Phoebe finally faced up to the fact that they were meant to be together, they'd been close friends for years. Though Phoebe was her friend as well, it wouldn't have surprised her if Phoebe passed on her secret annoyance with her virginity.

When Noah walked into Jake's office, it was like a livewire crackled between them. Heat flooded her, and she'd tried like crazy to keep it together. The absolute last thing she needed was for Jake to pick up on something and call Noah out in front of Dane and Hank. Lily sighed and brushed her hair away from her face. The line inched forward. They were in the longest, coldest part of Maine winter now, which meant the local hangouts tended to fill up with residents antsy from cabin fever.

The deli tables were filled. As she looked around, she felt a tap on her shoulder and turned around to find Phoebe behind her.

"Hey..." Her words were muffled when Phoebe tugged her into a quick hug.

"Hey yourself. I just said to Jake that I

hadn't seen you since we had dinner. How's it going?"

Lily shrugged. "Pretty good."

Phoebe waited expectantly, making her wonder what Phoebe knew. When Lily didn't say anymore, Phoebe's eyes narrowed. Conveniently, Lily was next up to order.

"It's my lucky day! You're both here at the same time." Roxanne's wide smile encompassed her and Phoebe before she focused on Lily. "What'll it be? Coffee, food, or something else?"

"I'm on a coffee run for Jake. He's meeting with Dane, Hank, and Noah..." Lily's words ran out when she saw Roxanne's grin widen. The last thing she needed was Roxanne cueing Phoebe in on her and Noah. Flushing like mad, Lily tried not to blush though she knew that was impossible. She didn't know if Roxanne would have enough sense to know she wasn't ready for the Phoebe to know about her and Noah yet. Not that she wanted to hide it from Phoebe, in fact she could use some advice, but if Phoebe knew, that meant Jake would know soon.

Roxanne chuckled and shook her head when she saw Lily's face. Lily sighed with relief inside when it appeared Roxanne was going to leave it be. Unfortunately, Phoebe was more observant than Lily would have liked and glanced between them.

"Okay, what's up?" Phoebe asked, her eyes swinging to Lily. "You were a little off the other night. I couldn't put my finger on it, and you're so damn private I didn't want to push you. Jake mentioned he thought something was up with you too. Spit it out. I won't go running to Jake if that's what you're worried about."

Lily looked between Roxanne and Phoebe. Roxanne shrugged apologetically. Phoebe's dark eyes were warm and concerned. Phoebe was one of the friends Lily usually turned to for advice and support, and she could seriously use both right about now. It wasn't that Lily didn't trust her not to tell Jake, but she knew how observant her brother was. Lily sighed. For better or worse, she needed to get this thing with Noah out in the open and somehow find a way to not be half-crazy with lust over him all the time. Not to mention finding a way to talk some sense into her heart. If her heart had its way, she and Noah were meant to be. *That's what you get for avoiding relationships for so long. The first guy you have sex with has you convinced he's the one and only. How would you even know better? Because what I have with Noah is so much more...* Her mind debated with itself. She was so out of her depth with Noah. Her limited experience with relationships in general wasn't the least helpful with the fact that she'd stumbled into the most earth-shattering, mind-blowing sex she could have ever imagined with a man who made her heart and body clench with the depth of her hopes and dreams.

She took a breath and met Phoebe's eyes again. "Can we get some coffee first?"

Phoebe grinned. Roxanne quickly took her order. When Phoebe stepped into the restroom, Roxanne turned back to Lily. "You can only keep a secret for so long around here. I didn't mean to give anything away, but maybe it's for the best."

Lily shrugged. "I wouldn't be worried if I could make sense of this thing with Noah."

Roxanne's eyes were warm. "You're over-thinking it." She turned away to adjust the espresso machine knobs and quickly finished getting the coffee order ready.

Lily snagged a table and sipped her coffee while she waited for Phoebe. Moments later, Phoebe sat down and looked expectantly at Lily.

Lily traced the edge of the lid on her coffee. The mere thought of talking about Noah kicked her pulse up a notch. "Well, the thing is...I've been seeing Noah." She paused and glanced over at Phoebe. Phoebe's eyes widened slightly, but she remained quiet.

"It's, um, kind of a lot. It happened fast, but I really like him and now I don't know what to do. I don't want Jake to get all protective and stuff, so it's not like I'm trying to hide it, it's just I don't know. Ugh." She rested her forehead in her palms for a moment before looking up. Phoebe's eyes were warm and soft.

"I think I'm in over my head here."

Phoebe's smile was slow in coming, but her glee was evident. "This is perfect! I wondered how long it would take you to get over yourself and give someone, anyone, a chance. Noah's seems like a great guy. Jake has nothing but good things to say about him lately. When did you start seeing him?"

Lily's face was so hot, she was surprised she didn't melt from embarrassment. "Just a few weeks ago," she mumbled. "I don't know what Noah thinks, but..."

Roxanne happened by their table right then and interjected. "If you're wondering what Noah thinks, he's in love with you."

Lily's head whipped up. Her heart clenched and hope crashed through her. *Please, please let that be true.* "How do you know?"

Roxanne grinned. "Because when I gave him a little lecture about how he'd better be good to you, that's what he said. I told you, you're overthinking this." Roxanne swung her gaze to Phoebe. "Noah's in here almost every day, so I've gotten to know him since he's been back in Catamount. He's head over heels for Lily. If you ask me, they're perfect for each other. Noah's just as private as Lily is and he's a total sweetheart. I mean, the guy came home to take care of his mother because she has cancer. Then there's the fact that's he's totally easy on the eyes and with a body to die for. Not like I have a thing for him, but you do," she said, meeting Lily's eyes with a mischievous grin.

Lily's figured her face might as well have been painted bright red at this point while her heart threatened to pound its way out of her chest. Noah told Roxanne he loved her? She was almost afraid to believe it. She wanted to run back to Jake's office and drag Noah outside to hear him say it himself.

"Well, if I was wondering how you felt about him, I'm not anymore," Phoebe said wryly.

Lily swung her eyes back to Phoebe, her face getting even hotter. "I...ugh. I'm terrible at this. I don't know. Half the time I think I'm crazy, and the other half—I can't stop thinking about him." She nervously twirled her hair around her finger and took a gulp of coffee, savoring the heat of it.

Someone called Roxanne's name. She turned to holler she'd be right over and turned back to Lily. "Just like I said, you're overthinking it." She caught Phoebe's gaze. "Tell her. You did the same damn thing over Jake for years." At that, Roxanne leaned down and tugged Lily into a swift hug before striding away, filling coffees as she moved through the deli.

Phoebe waited a beat before speaking. "Since this is the first I've heard of it, I can't say I know a whole lot about what's going on between you two, but I know the look I saw on your face. It perfectly captured how I felt about Jake before we finally sorted things out. I don't know Noah too well myself, but

Roxanne's judgment is rock solid. If she thinks he's a good guy, he is." Phoebe paused, her eyes assessing. "I don't mean to be too nosy, but does Noah know you're..."

Lily put her face in her hands. "Oh. My. God. You're seriously gonna go there? I can't believe I ever told you that. I know you're the one who told Jake too, which is half the reason I'm worried about how he's going to react." She dropped her hands and eyed Phoebe. "Yes, Noah knows I *was* a virgin. That's not an issue."

Phoebe had the grace to look chagrined. "I didn't mean to make it sound like it was a problem, but you were kind of stressing about it. As for Jake, it slipped out one time when we were talking. I wish like hell it hadn't because you're right. He's pretty damn protective when it comes to you." Her moment of chagrin passed when her eyes widened. "Wait a minute? Did I hear you right?"

Lily sighed. "Yes. I said 'was.' Not that I still am."

A slow grin spread across Phoebe's face.

"Well, well. Noah was the magic charm, huh?"

The blush that wouldn't quit kept getting hotter. Lily didn't bother to reply and only shrugged.

Phoebe chuckled. "Fine then. Well, as worried as you were about it, I'm happy that's all taken care of now. Not that you're asking me, but I think the sooner you tell Jake about Noah, the better. Let him know how you feel and tell him to back off."

Lily sighed, her tension easing slightly. Phoebe had a point. "I'm with you there. Honestly, it'd be easier if I wasn't so insane over Noah. I wish I had more experience with men. I can't stop thinking about him. But how do I know it's as good as I think it is?"

Phoebe rolled her eyes and sighed. "Maybe I dated a little more than you did, but honestly, you don't know something's good until you have it. The way you look when you talk about him tells me it's good. It sounds like he feels the same way, so I'm with Roxanne on this one. Stop overthinking it."

Lily took a breath and nodded slowly. She wished she could reconcile her mixed feelings about being a shifter with everything. Somehow, falling for Noah the way she was rubbed against her anxiety about it. She worried she was letting her emotions run the show. She'd seen shifter relationships blow up in spectacular fashion. As deeply as she felt for Noah, it would be devastating if that happened. "Easier said than done, but I'll try. I think I'll talk to Jake about it this afternoon. I'll let you know how it goes."

11

Noah stood with his back to the door, straining to stay calm. Jake paced in front of him, his hand slashing through the air with every word.

"Did you think you could hide this from me? She's my sister! The second I saw you look at her when she asked you what kind of coffee you wanted, I knew."

Jake stopped in front of him and whirled to face him. "Tell me now how long this has been going on and what the hell your intentions are?" Jake was vibrating with anger.

Noah didn't think it would be particularly helpful if he was too direct about how he felt—Lily turned him inside out, his body needed her as much as it needed air. He'd do anything for her. No, he thought perhaps that wasn't how he should word his feelings when it came to Jake. He heard footsteps coming up the path to the door and then the door pushed against his back. He stepped out of the way. Hank and Dane had left a few minutes ago. Lily came through the door carrying a holder with coffees for all of them, including the now departed Hank and Dane. Her eyes bounced between them. She took a deep breath and set the coffees on Jake's desk before turning to him.

"What the hell is going on?" she demanded.

Jake glared at her. "Were you planning to mention whatever the hell is going on between you and Noah here?" he asked, pointing at Noah, his eyes hard and cold.

Lily's cheeks flushed, but she didn't back down. "In what world do I have to report to my big brother when I get involved with someone?"

Jake swore and rolled his eyes. "You're my only sister. I get to be protective. Plus, why do you need to hide anything?"

Lily threw her hands up. "Because I was afraid you'd act like this." She turned to Noah. "Did he threaten you?"

Noah shook his head, figuring the less he said, the better.

She swung back to Jake, her hands on her hips and her eyes flashing. "I'm twenty-eight years old, Jake. Just like you can go about your business with Phoebe without giving me and everyone else a blow by blow, so can I. I meant to talk to you about Noah soon anyway. Don't be an ass. He means a lot to me. Don't you dare blame him for not saying anything to you because that's my call, not his."

Noah's chest was tight. Hearing Lily's quick defense of him and declaration that he meant a lot to her nearly choked him up. It was entirely unnecessary for her to step in to protect him from Jake's wrath. He figured Jake was pissed not because he thought he had the right to say who could or couldn't be with his sister, but because he cared about his sister and wanted to make sure she was with someone good enough for her. Noah could only hope he was—because every day that passed made it more and more difficult to imagine life without her.

He squared his shoulders and cleared his throat. "I get why you'd be concerned about me. Seems like you want to make sure Lily's with someone good enough for her. I can't say if I am, but I love her and I'd do anything for her." His words came out rough, but he kept his gaze on Jake. His heart pounded because he didn't quite know if Lily felt for him what he felt for her. His instincts told him she did, but instinct could be weak against the vagaries of mind and emotions. But he wasn't going to hide behind his fear with Jake.

Jake met Noah's eyes. The anger in his expression eased, if only slightly. The silence was heavy as Jake considered him. Jake's gaze traveled back to Lily, a question in his eyes. Noah couldn't see Lily's face, but whatever Jake saw there caused him to nod firmly. He turned back to Noah. "You love her, huh?"

Noah nodded. This was definitely not the way he'd have chosen to tell Lily how he felt, but he wasn't going to shy away. Jake remained silent for another beat before swinging away to lean against his desk.

"Don't suppose I need to say this, but if you hurt her..."

Lily stepped in front of Jake and lightly pushed against his chest. "Oh my God! Is that necessary? What if I'm the one that hurts

Noah? It's so ridiculous for you to be all tough like this."

Jake's expression softened as he chuckled. "You're not going to hurt Noah. You have a heart of gold. If he didn't mean a lot to you, you wouldn't be standing here getting in the middle of this. You can act like it's because I'm your brother, and maybe it is, but any of your friends would kick his ass if he hurt you. Phoebe would be first in line."

Lily threw her hands up and snatched her coffee out of the holder. "Whatever." She swung around to face Noah. His heart tightened, his breath became shallow, and lust surged through his veins. Lily was like a direct line drug to his heart and body. All of it was mixed together—love, lust, and everything else that was Lily.

She took a swallow of coffee, her blue eyes on him. "Are you done here?"

Noah managed to nod. Relieved as he was that the cat was out of the bag, so to speak, he still didn't want to get a hard on in front of Jake. He forced himself to look away from Lily to Jake. "I'll touch base after I visit Theo and see if he'll talk."

At Jake's nod, he paused and gathered himself. "Look, I hope you know I wasn't trying to be sleazy and pull one over on you about Lily. I know she means a lot to you. Things just...happened. I wanted it to be her choice to talk to you about it, but it is what it is."

Jake looked between them, a rueful smile passing over his face. "I get it. Hope you understand where I was coming from."

The respect Noah had for Jake only increased as a result of Jake's protectiveness of Lily. Noah nodded and turned away. Lily snagged his coffee and handed it to him. "You might as well get your coffee before its cold."

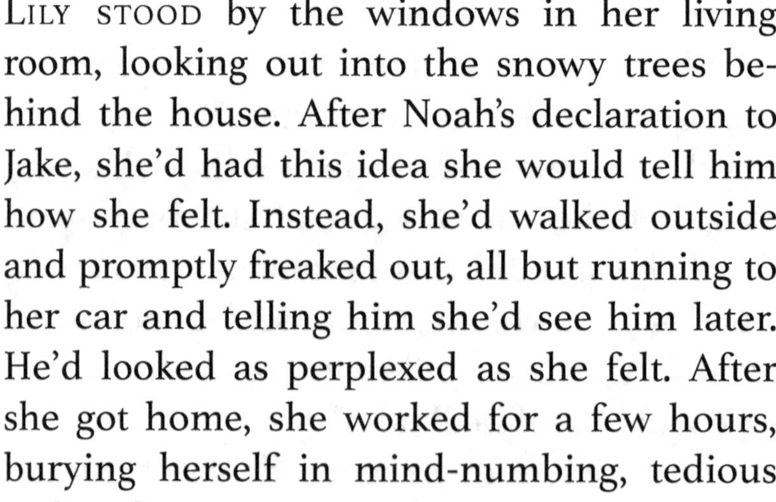

LILY STOOD by the windows in her living room, looking out into the snowy trees behind the house. After Noah's declaration to Jake, she'd had this idea she would tell him how she felt. Instead, she'd walked outside and promptly freaked out, all but running to her car and telling him she'd see him later. He'd looked as perplexed as she felt. After she got home, she worked for a few hours, burying herself in mind-numbing, tedious coding fixes.

It was late afternoon now with the sun beginning its slow bow. It was sliding down behind the trees, lavender and pink streaking the sky in its wake. A cardinal landed on a tree branch nearby, a flash of color in the fading light. Lily's phone dinged. Pulling it out of her pocket, a text from Noah blinked at her.

Can I stop by?

Lily flushed, even though she was standing all by herself. She was embarrassed she hadn't found the courage to let Noah know how she felt right then and there. It was all too much with Jake's interference. Since this afternoon, she couldn't think clearly. She needed some space. Noah was taking up almost all of it in her heart and mind, and she was afraid she was jumping in too quickly. She didn't know if she could do it, but she resolved that she was going to tell him she needed some time. Her feelings were too much, too intense, and like nothing she'd ever experienced. *Noah stood right in front of you and told your brother he loved you, and this is what you give him in return? I can't. Not yet.*

She took a breath before replying to Noah.

I'm in the middle of some stuff for work.

She felt like a coward, but she needed some way to get her head clear. It would be impossible if Noah were near.

His reply was brief. *Okay.*

Her heart pounded, anxiety knotted in her chest. She fell asleep later, wondering if she'd just gone and ruined the best thing that ever happened to her.

12

———————

Several days later, Noah woke alone in his bed. As soon as he became conscious, he thought of Lily and felt almost sick. He didn't know what had happened between those moments in her brother's office and the other night, but she shut him out. His heart ached, and he felt like a fool. He'd laid his feelings bare, but it hadn't even mattered. He kicked the covers back and forced himself to get up. A while later, he walked down the hall to check on his mother. After a quick knock on her bedroom door, he heard a faint reply. He pushed the door open and found his mother sitting in bed, propped up on her pillows reading.

Carol glanced up at him. "Hi there." Her

eyes were weary, but then his mother had carried an edge of weariness for as long as he could remember. Being married to his father was beyond exhausting. Noah hated that she had to face cancer now. He wanted her to be able to enjoy the time she had now that his father wasn't around to constantly belittle, berate, and beat on her.

He swatted those thoughts away and summoned a smile. "Hey Mom, how're you feeling this morning?"

Her shoulder rose and fell elegantly. "As well as can be expected." She held his eyes, her gaze expectant. He knew she noticed something because she'd always tuned into him easily.

"What?" he asked.

"Are you okay?" Her soft question nudged at his sore heart and wounded pride.

He shrugged. "I'm not sure what's up with Lily. I told her I loved her, and she's blowing me off now."

Carol's eyes widened and she took a breath. Her eyes met his, warmth and concern in them. "I haven't mentioned it because I know how private you are, but Roxanne told me about you two. It sounds like she means a lot to you."

Noah sat on the edge of his mother's bed and laced his hands together. "She does. I, uh, didn't think I'd ever feel this way about someone. I never wanted to after I saw the way Dad treated you..."

His mother shook her head. "What I had with your father wasn't love. That marriage came out of a young girl who didn't have enough sense to catch onto the kind of man your father was before it was too late. I've worried for years you'd never give love a chance, and it broke my heart because you're everything I ever wanted in a son. Most of all, you're a good man with a heart of gold."

Tears choked his throat. He took a labored breath as he turned and met his mother's eyes. "Maybe you should give yourself most of the credit for that. You taught me what love was."

His mother's eyes brightened with tears. She held a hand out. He grabbed it and squeezed tightly before letting go.

"Not so sure it's going to matter right now," he said, a bitter edge to his words.

His mother sighed. "Noah, things aren't always as they seem. From what I know of Lily, she hasn't really been involved with anyone. A bump in the road doesn't mean anything more than that. Love does funny things to people. Even the best of us act in the worst ways to the ones we love the most. Give her a little space and see what happens."

He took a breath, trying to loosen the tight feeling in his chest and ease the fear galloping through him. Lily meant so much to him, it almost scared him. He nodded firmly. "Right. I'll try."

After a heavy pause, he looked to her again. "You haven't mentioned when your next chemo treatment is."

"Next week. You know, I can get there on my own."

"I know. I don't take you because I think you can't. I want to be there with you."

She nodded slowly. "Okay then. Time for a change of topic. Wallace Peyton called me yesterday."

"What?" Noah all but barked the question.

Carol arched a brow and chuckled. "Honey, you don't need to worry about Wallace intimidating me. I'm dying of cancer. It's very freeing, if you think about it."

"Mom, stop saying you're dying. You don't know that for sure." He had to beat back the anxiety with fear hot on its heels. His mother was one of the best parts of his life. Even though he'd kept himself at a distance until his father died, she'd been the rock that anchored him inside.

She held his eyes steadily. "Maybe it's not official, but it's a matter of time. I know it's hard for you to hear, but it's easier for me if I face it. But that's not what I wanted to talk about. Wallace is who I wanted to talk about."

"What the hell did he say?"

His mother threw him a disapproving look, but refrained from comment. She was one of the most polite people he knew. Swearing was generally not part of her vocabulary.

He shrugged, slightly abashed.

"Well, he was hoping someone could talk some sense into you about your involvement with Jake and Hank. He spouted some bullshit about how you don't really know the whole story. As if I'm that stupid. Lord knows why he thought I'd be helpful. Wallace has always been way too confident of his influence. I doubt it ever occurred to him I could care less about what happens to him. Do me a favor though."

"Anything."

"Be careful."

~

"You know, I've been doing my damnedest to keep my mouth shut about Noah, but I'm done," Jake declared.

Lily stood inside the house Jake shared with Phoebe and stared at him. She crossed her arms over her chest, trying to hold herself together. She couldn't say just yet that she knew deep down she'd made a huge mistake. All she'd meant to do was find a little breathing room, but now she couldn't seem to figure out how to bridge the distance she'd created. Every time she thought about Noah, her heart ached. She took a breath and forced herself to look at her brother.

"Okay then, what's so important you can't stay out of it?" she asked defiantly.

Phoebe caught her eyes, a look of concern in them. Lily ignored her. She'd given Phoebe a ride home since her car was in the shop.

Jake leaned against the counter and held her eyes steadily. "I'll admit I was pissed about Noah at first, but he manned up and told me exactly how much you meant to him right then and there. Take it from me, but I know that wasn't easy for him to do. He hasn't said a word to me, but it's obvious something's up. I've seen him every day the last few days and he can barely look at me if I say your name. I finally pushed him on it today, and he told me you're not talking to him. What the hell is wrong with you?"

Flustered, Lily started to pace back and forth in the small kitchen. "I don't know. It all happened so fast. I just needed a little time..."

"Time for what?" Jake countered.

"To make sure I wasn't just letting my stupid shifter feelings take over!"

Jake's eyes widened, and Phoebe swung to Lily, her gaze shocked.

"What the hell do you mean?" Jake demanded.

Lily threw her hands up. "Just that. It's all emotion, no reason. I can't think straight. It seems too much, too fast, too...everything. I've never had a relationship before, so maybe I should take a step back and make sure I'm not falling into this because it's so new and exciting."

Jake stared at her incredulously. "Lily, you know," his words thudded against her, "that you can't deny what your shifter wants. Trust me, I tried it for years. It was only when I finally listened to what I knew all along about Phoebe that I started to feel better."

Her stomach churned as she stared at him. "It's not always like that though. When shifters break up, it's ugly, crazy drama."

Phoebe spoke up. "Lily, I don't think Jake means every relationship shifters have is the one that's meant to be. I think he's talking about when you know the other person or shifter is the right and only one for you." She looked to Jake. "Right?"

He nodded tightly. "And that's exactly what I feel with you and Noah. It's so obvious, I can't believe you're doing this."

Lily stood there, trying to take his words in, but she was annoyed with his interference, the fact that he thought he knew what was in her heart. She whirled away and almost ran out the door. As she drove home, tears rolled down her cheeks.

A SHARP KNOCK came on the kitchen door. Noah stood up from the kitchen table and opened the door. Jake stood on the other side.

"Mind if I come in?" he asked.

Noah stepped back and gestured for Jake to come in. Noah's mother was out running errands. Noah checked the coffee pot and held it up in question. Jake shook his head.

"Have a seat," Noah said as he slid back into a chair by the kitchen table.

Jake sat across from him. He was quiet for a long moment.

"Everything okay?" Noah finally asked, uncertain why Jake stopped by.

Jake idly traced a circle on the table before speaking. "You might think it's none of my business, but it's about Lily."

Noah's throat tightened and his heart thudded painfully. He really didn't want to discuss Lily with Jake. His feelings were too fresh, too raw. But he couldn't quite figure a way out of it. Jake's eyes were on him. He finally nodded.

"Maybe I came across a bit strong when I first heard about you and Lily, but I think you're a good guy. I, uh, thought I might let you know Lily can be stubborn."

Noah's mouth twisted and his breath came out in a huff. "I could've guessed that."

Jake chuckled softly before his gaze sobered again. "Look, Lily's got her back up about this, and I think I made things worse. I tried to talk to her, and it only pissed her off. I wouldn't have said anything if it weren't for what I saw when you two were in the same room."

Noah's gut churned and he took a gulp of air. "And you came to tell me this because...?"

"Because I think if you go talk to her, maybe it'll help." Jake grimaced apologetically and shrugged.

"You think I should go talk to her? She's the one who told me she needed space!"

"I know, I know. Look, you didn't watch me go through this, but it took me too damn long, like years, to face up to how much Phoebe meant to me. Our family has a stubborn streak that can be self-destructive. I know Lily loves you. I thought maybe if she saw you face to face, she'd stop getting in her own way."

Noah ran a hand through his hair and sighed. "I'll think about it."

Jake nodded slowly. "Good enough for me."

13

———

Lily stared out her windows. She'd been doing that way too much the last few days. Twilight was falling, and she felt lonely. She missed Noah. She mined inside for the courage to call him, but she was flustered and felt stupid. A tiny corner of her mind knew her pride was getting in the way. With a sigh, she swung away from the windows and went to stare at the contents of her refrigerator. She was hungry, but nothing seemed appealing and she hadn't bothered to shop this week. Her phone beeped, indicating a text had arrived. Her heart started pounding when she saw it was from Noah.

Mind if I stop by?

Did she mind? No! Relief washed over her, so hard and fast she could hardly breathe. Tears spring to her eyes. She forced herself to close her eyes and made a feeble attempt to gather herself together. Pulse racing, she typed her reply.

Of course. When?

Now?

That's fast.

I'm standing at your door.

She whirled around and almost ran to the door. Flinging it open, cold air gusted into the room. Noah stood there, his amber eyes locked on her. He was everything he'd always been—tall, dark, handsome and so damn sexy her breath hitched and her pulse ran wild simply looking at him. Now that she'd gotten to know the man he was, her heart was in as deep as her body. She was so overwhelmed with emotion, she just gaped at him. He arched a brow when she stood frozen in the doorway.

She took a quick step back, mumbling half-formed words. He stepped through the door, shutting it behind him. She hugged her arms around her waist, trying to corral the sensations running through her body. That sweet electricity hummed to life between them. She forced herself to let her arms go and look up at him. The look in his eyes reached out and grabbed hold of her heart. Without a word, he closed the small distance between them, his hand lacing into her hair as he held her gaze.

His eyes fell closed and he rested his forehead against hers. A ripple ran through her. He slid an arm around her, his hand sliding in a firm stroke up her back. She felt enveloped in warmth and strength. Her pulse raced though her heart started to settle. She breathed him in—the clean scent he carried, snow and the barest hint of wood smoke.

Desire curled around them, but Lily wasn't going to let herself get swept away without making sure Noah knew what lay inside her heart. She leaned back, tilting her face up to his. He moved back just far enough for her to see his eyes. Her heart pounded and her belly clenched.

She forced herself to speak past her anxiety. "I'm sorry I shut you out. I, um...this is all new to me. The shifter in me felt so strongly, I got scared I wasn't being rational. Then..." She paused and took a gulp of air. Her heart was beating so fast, she was speaking too quickly, her words running away from her.

Before she could form another word, he started sifting through her hair. "I meant what I said, you know. I love you. I wake up thinking about you and fall asleep thinking about you. I'm not about to play like it's anything other than what it is. I want everything with you, and I'll wait as long as I have to until you're ready."

Her heart flew skyward. She felt like the sun had come out after days of rain. His eyes were on her, waiting. "In case you didn't notice, I haven't had a ton of experience with anything like this. I wanted tell you I loved you too, but I blew it. I freaked out. My brain got in the way like it always does."

As soon as the words left her mouth, they felt so right and true, her chest almost burst with the wash of feeling. She started to take a steadying breath when his lips crashed against hers. In a flash, she was swept into the dizzying passion between them. Just as swiftly, he gentled his kiss, drawing away. He whispered against her lips, his breath mingling with hers.

"Well, that's good then. I was ready to be stoic, but it would've been the hardest thing I ever did." He chuckled softly and drew back further. His hand loosened in her hair, his thumb stroking the soft skin behind her ear, sending shivers through her entire body. Staring into the warm amber of his eyes suffused her body with heat. She struggled to catch her breath. His lips brushed across hers quickly before he took a step back.

"I had to come over and see you, but truth is, I'm starving."

Lily giggled, her emotions so keyed up, she couldn't stop laughing once she started. When she finally caught her breath, she looked over to find Noah watching her, his expression amused.

"Wasn't trying to be funny there."

His stomach growled audibly, and she giggled again.

"Okay, let's go eat somewhere. I'd offer to cook, but I forgot to go to the grocery store this week, so our options are limited here."

"The Trailhead?"

She nodded firmly and stepped to the door, stuffing her feet in her boots and throwing her jacket on.

NOAH WOKE IN THE DARK. Lily lay half atop him, her legs tangled in his and her breasts against his side. Moonlight fell through the window, limning her skin in a silvery glow. Rolling his head to the side, he saw that it was snowing outside, the snowflakes glittering as if they were stardust. He ran his hand down Lily's back, coming to rest on the generous curve of her bottom. She shifted against him, all softness and warmth. His body stirred—again. He chuckled to himself. He'd prided himself on his physical discipline and control—a necessary aspect of his success in the military. Along came Lily and she shattered his control simply by existing. He fell back asleep to the rhythm of her breathing.

14

———

A few days later, Noah recalled his mother's request that he be careful. He looked out through the trees into a quarry. He was in lion form, hidden from view in the trees. Jake and Dane were nearby, also perched in the trees. They watched and waited. His days had been filled with unraveling the last of the secrets Callen Peyton left behind. His nights had been consumed with Lily—sense-stealing, heart clenching and devastating passion filled the hours with her. When they weren't twined together, he enjoyed the funny sweetness of her personality, and her jaunty independence. She flashed through his mind now. His lion coiled with tension at the thought of her. He forced himself to focus on the moment at hand.

To Noah's surprise, Theo had ended up talking to him and set the wheels in motion to take Wallace Peyton down. Theo had come to the conclusion that he'd be an easy mark to take the fall, so he opted to talk instead. In sum, while Callen was the one who originally stumbled upon the shifter smuggling network, Wallace had quickly stepped in and led the organization. Wallace had offered to have Catamount shifters smuggle drugs straight into Maine and elsewhere in New England where they'd be distributed throughout the East from there. Callen died on that highway in Connecticut in a failed attempt to prove shifters could safely navigate close to New York City. Connecticut shared the border with New York and was a tiny state with much of its border filled with urban commuters into New York.

Noah still couldn't quite believe how stupid and greedy Callen's plan had been. Outside of the northern portions of New England, where Catamount happened to be located, most of the Northeast was heavily populated with several large urban areas, New York City included. The plan would have brought gobs of money to Wallace and anyone involved because of the price to pay for the risk and the massive payoff of getting a direct connection to the East. Callen's death hadn't swayed Wallace. Theo may not have had much pull, but he'd danced along the edge of what was legal for so many years, he had connections. Without Wallace, the smuggling pipeline would shut down in Catamount. No one else in Catamount had the resources to pull it off. Noah had enough sense to know this would only be a temporary setback, but it would at least clear the air in Catamount for the time being.

With Hank's and his police force in place for backup, Noah, Jake and Dane were out at the quarry waiting for a planned delivery. Derek had agreed to ostensibly cave in to Kirk's demands to use the quarry, so they could hopefully catch Wallace and his crew in the act. This would be the first actual delivery from the shifters out West. Jake had hacked into Wallace's email and phone accounts and tracked communications. Wallace had promised to be on site for this since it would be the first successful delivery if all went as planned.

Noah scented movement in the trees to

the far side of the quarry. He glanced to the side and saw Jake and Dane with their eyes trained in the same direction. As they watched, a pair of mountain lions stepped out from the trees and moved quietly across the field to the edge of the quarry. What appeared to be an abandoned moving vehicle sat by one of the quarry walls. Tall cliffs surrounded the quarry, creating a natural shield. Noah, Jake and Dane had chosen this side because it was situated lower where they could see into the quarry. The lions waited in the cold. The sky was slate gray, the air damp and cold. The sound of tires on gravel broke through the quiet.

Brad's truck appeared with Brad and Wallace inside. They parked nearby and climbed out. Conveniently, they parked in such a way that they shielded the view of the trees. After a shared glance, Noah, Jake and Dane stealthily climbed down from the trees. Once Brad and Wallace began unloading crates from the moving vehicle and examining them, they made their move. Bolting across the field, Noah exalted in the rush of power and strength. Running in lion form was an experience of pure power and exhilaration. He barreled straight forward, Jake and Dane on pace with him, until they separated when they reached the vehicles. Wallace and Brad, shockingly, hadn't heard their approach. They were pre-occupied with prying open the crates to confirm the delivery. The two shifters who'd been waiting ahead swung in their direction.

As planned, Noah and Jake targeted Brad and Wallace while Dane distracted the other two. If they could overpower Brad and Wallace, they'd retain the advantage. If not, they were outnumbered. Noah dashed at Wallace who shifted at the last second, but not in time to stave off Noah's attack. Noah knocked him to the ground. Wallace was swift and fought back viciously. The next few minutes were a blur of motion, snarls and growls. Brad didn't share the fight his father had and was more easily dispatched. Jake briefly joined Noah's battle with Wallace, but backed off when Noah managed to pin Wallace again. Dane had taken a swipe and dodge approach with the two shifters from out of town, leading them on weaving loops in and out of the trees. When he saw Jake headed his direction, he chased them back into the quarry with the help of Derek who'd been waiting at another vantage point deeper in the woods.

The plan had been for Hank and his crew to surround the quarry and prevent anyone from bolting the area, but preferably, they'd be able to stay in human form for the purposes of handling the arrests without getting caught up in lion fights. Once Derek joined them, Noah could ease his grip on Wallace's neck. Wallace was a proud man and lion. Although he was injured, he stood before he shifted back into human form. Without a glance, he calmly gathered his torn clothing and put himself together. He moved with a pronounced limp. His eyes met Noah's—they held anger, but a hint of respect. When Wallace glanced to Brad, his lip curled in a sneer. Brad was clearly not the son he'd expected. Brad ignored his father.

The next few hours passed rapidly. Hank led the police in to confiscate the deliveries and left with Wallace, Brad and their two accomplices in cuffs. Noah recognized one of them must be Carl Jasper because he looked so much like Theo, it was startling.

LATE THAT NIGHT, Noah walked quietly into his mother's house. Lily was waiting at her home for him to stop by. She'd called and texted every hour since he'd notified her Wallace had finally been arrested.

"Hey Mom," he called softly as he closed the kitchen door behind him.

She sat at the kitchen table reading on the new tablet he'd gotten her. She loved to read, but often complained of the light, so he'd gotten her a tablet in the hopes she'd find it easier. After ignoring it for weeks, she finally tried it and hadn't gone anywhere without it since. She looked up and smiled, standing when he reached her side.

She tugged him in for a hug and kissed him on the cheek, her palm stroking his face. "How come you didn't go straight to Lily? I've already gotten the entire story from Roxanne. She called me once she heard the news."

Noah chuckled. "Should've known. I just wanted to make sure you knew I was okay and see how you were feeling."

Carol sat back down and grinned at him. "I'm feeling just fine. I've got a new book here, so there's no need for you to worry. Get out of here and find your girl." She waved him off and went back to reading.

A short drive later, he pulled up at Lily's house. She met him at the door and yanked him inside. He hadn't had time to clean up, so she immediately exclaimed over his appearance and looked him over.

She nudged the edge of his collar out of the way, her finger following a scratch down. "Am I going to find you all torn up under this shirt?"

Her blue eyes snagged his, concerned and bright with tears. He caught her hand in his. "A few scratches, but I'm fine. No need to worry."

He dipped his head down and caught her mouth in a kiss. Her breath came out in a sigh, and he delved into the warm sweetness of her mouth. Lust jolted through him. Adrenaline was still pumping through his veins from this afternoon. He tugged her roughly against him. Suddenly, all he needed was to be inside of her *now*. He tore at her shirt and shoved her jeans down. She matched his intensity, yanking his clothes off. Clothing was strewn about them on the floor. He hadn't taken more than a step away from the door. He turned and backed her against it. His cock throbbed. Her soft skin gave under his touch. She gasped at his roughness, writhing and flexing in his embrace.

He hooked a hand under her thigh, lifting it high, and delved into her drenched folds. He groaned against her mouth and tore his lips away. He needed to see her face. Her cheeks were flushed, her hair a messy tangle. Her blue eyes were dark, her lips parted. Her pulse fluttered in her neck. He stroked a finger through her wetness, and she gasped. He stroked again...and again... and again. Her hips shifted restlessly against his touch. He finally plunged his fingers inside of her. She cried out, her eyes falling closed as her head rolled against the door.

He couldn't wait anymore and dragged his fingers out, coasting across her clit. She arched into his touch. He stepped the cradle of her hips and rocked against her. Her eyes flew wide and slammed into his.

"Now," he whispered.

He nudged the head of his cock into her folds and held still, forcing himself to wait. Her body vibrated in his arms, straining toward him. He surged into the creamy clench of her channel. His breath broke on a groan. Her eyes held his, their faces mere inches apart. He began to stroke into and out of the warm, silken pressure of her. Her breath hummed, her body tensed quickly and she cried out abruptly, his name falling from her lips in a broken chant. As she throbbed around him, he let loose, his orgasm crashing through him, on the edge of violence. The release was so intense, his knees buckled for a moment. When he finally came to, it was to the feel of Lily's breasts rising and falling against his chest in rhythm with his own breath.

EPILOGUE

Weeks later, Noah sat beside his mother in the waiting room at the hospital. She was on her way into another round of chemo. Today, she was barely paying attention to him. Lily had asked if she could join them. At the moment, she was busy talking with his mother. He leaned his head back against the wall and sighed. He couldn't have fathomed that the simple act of her coming to this appointment with him would break down another wall for him, but his heart clenched so tight, he was on the verge of tears.

Later that afternoon, his mother looked across the kitchen table and shook her head.

"Noah, I don't want to move in with you and Lily. I'm perfectly comfortable here, and I truly enjoy the peace and quiet. You need to start your life with her."

"Mom, I don't want you to be alone. What if you need something? If you really want to stay here, I'll talk to Lily and we can just wait."

Carol angled her head to the side. "Stop trying to make up for what your father did and stop feeling guilty for moving away until after he died."

"Mom..."

She put a hand up. "I know you. I know it's been weighing on you, but let it go. I was so happy when you got out from under your father's thumb. As awful as this mess with the drug smuggling has been for Catamount, I'm glad for what it gave you. You left here and climbed right through the ranks into the Special Forces, but whenever you were in Catamount, you acted like none of that mattered. The way you helped with everything gave you a chance to see no one here held your father against you. For that, I'm glad. As for where I stay, I'm staying right here, and I will *not* tolerate you trying to delay your time with Lily."

He gave his mother a long look and sighed. A tension he hadn't known he'd been holding left his body. He couldn't change the past, but he could change the future and re-member the past was only part of his story.

Later that evening, he watched Lily chop vegetables and stir them into a pan. He'd dis-covered she was quite the cook though she demurred. He slipped his hand in his pocket and tugged out a tiny box. In the spirit of looking forward, he decided he wouldn't shy away from the one thing that still gave him a jolt of fear: marriage, or even thinking about marriage. When he'd said as much to his mother, she asked him how he'd feel if there was any question about his commitment to Lily. He'd started to argue with her when he realized that was precisely her point.

"If you dance around the idea of mar-riage because of your father, then you're let-ting him still have power over you."

His mother's words echoed in his mind as he turned the tiny box in his hands. He'd fi-nagled Roxanne's company with him to Port-land to find a ring for Lily. He removed the ring from the box, sliding the box back in his pocket. The ring sat like a burning coal in his palm. Lily wasn't much for stones, so he'd gone with a simple platinum band with Roxanne's firm approval. His heart was pounding as he looked over at Lily. She was preoccupied with tossing the stir-fry she was making. Her hair was tied in a loose ponytail, which hung haphazardly to the side. She must have sensed him looking her way because she glanced up.

"What?" she asked.

He pushed away from the counter. Stopping in front of her, where she stood with a spatula in one hand and her blue eyes bright, he took a breath. He tried to form words, but he couldn't. Instead, he simply held his palm out. Her eyes canted down and immediately flew up to his again. His lack of speech was mirrored by hers. A sheen of tears glimmered in her eyes.

She finally spoke. "Oh my. Does this mean...?"

The capacity for speech returned. "It means I want everything. That includes making sure you know I'm one hundred percent committed to you."

The spatula clattered to the floor when Lily threw her arms around him. He caught her in his grip and held her close, breathing in the soft scents of her—a hint of vanilla and honey. When she pulled back, her smile trembled. She bit her lip, a tinge of shyness in her eyes. When she didn't say anything, his heart tightened, worrying he'd moved too fast.

"It's okay if..."

"Yes. That's all. Yes."

Relief followed by a hard, bright joy flashed through him.

LILY LOOKED out across the room. She'd decided it was time to have a gathering for friends now that she and Noah were officially together. Noah had moved in a few weeks ago. He insisted on stopping by to check on his mother every day, one of the many reasons Lily loved him. Noah stood by the kitchen counter, his hips resting against it while he talked with Jake and Dane.

His dark curls were messy, as usual. She still couldn't quite believe Noah Jasper was hers. Her wildest youthful fantasies couldn't have prepared her for what the real man was like. Tall, dark, handsome, and so sexy he brought her to her knees. She started toward him when Phoebe caught her elbow. "Is Shana coming tonight?"

Lily glanced around the room. "She said she would be here." A thread of worry formed. "Have you heard from her today?"

Phoebe shook her head. "Ever since they finally finished the investigation in Catamount, she's been, I don't know, off. I think she's relieved it's over, but now she doesn't have anything to focus on. The way Callen died and what he left behind hasn't been easy for her."

Lily sighed. "I know. All we can do is be there for her."

As she looked over the room, Noah's eyes caught hers. A current arced to life between them. Phoebe shook her head and smiled wryly. "I'll check on Shana later. In the meantime, you better get over there. You two are the worst."

"The worst at what?"

"At looking like you're about to go up in flames just by looking at each other."

Phoebe nudged her with her shoulder, and Lily crossed the room to Noah's side. In the weeks since Wallace was arrested, along with the rest of his local accomplices, things had started to settle in town, but the re-maining concern came from Montana. Ac-cording to Jake and Noah, Jake's contact out there had confirmed the network remained strong in that area. As far as they could tell, the Catamount end had been shut down. Lily couldn't bring herself to think past the moment, but worry lingered. Thinking of Shana brought it to the fore.

When she reached Noah's side, he slid his arm around her waist and tugged her close. Her body tingled all over, a warm current buzzing to life inside. Her brother had the sense to gracefully depart the con-versation with Dane following. She looked up at Noah, colliding with his amber gaze, which sent sparks skittering through her, igniting the embers of the fire that never died.

"So..." he said, arching a brow.

"So, what?"

"Have we been social long enough? I need you. *Now*. It's not too convenient with a house full of people."

Lily's belly clenched and moisture pooled between her thighs. It was that bad with him. She bit her lip and nodded. He dipped his head and brushed his lips across her quickly.

"So which one of us has a headache?" he asked.

She giggled and flushed straight through.

An hour or so later, she fell against him. His skin was damp, as was hers. Their breathing echoed through the bedroom. Her body felt liquid, sated beyond pliancy. Noah's palm stroked in circles on her back. Moonlight fell through the windows onto the bed, making the space feel magical, suspended in time. The last thing she remembered was the feel of his lips pressed against the curve of her neck before she fell asleep.

Thank you for reading Fated Mate - I hope you loved Lily & Noah's story!

For more steamy, small town shifter romance, Shana & Hayden's story is next in Destined Mate. Shana is trying to pick up the pieces of her life after her husband's tragic death and the discovery of his betrayal of Catamount shifters. The only man who seems capable of cracking through the ice is Hayden —a sexy, smoldering, and powerful shifter from Montana. Don't miss Hayden's story!

Keep reading for a sneak peek!

Be sure to sign up for my newsletter for the latest news, teasers & more! Click here to sign up: http://jhcroixauthor.com/subscribe/

EXCERPT: DESTINED MATE BY J.H. CROIX; ALL RIGHTS RESERVED

Shana Ashworth gritted her teeth as her feet slipped out from under her and she skidded onto the icy road. When her hip crashed against the pavement, she couldn't hold back her grunt. The pain seared through her. She unceremoniously came to a stop in the bramble of a bush beside the road, a bush that just happened to be wild rose with plenty of thorns on its bare branches. The early spring morning had tempted her for a run, and this is what she got for it.

Her breath misted in the cool air. She remained where she was for the moment. The bare ground peeked out from the lingering snow cover. She leaned back on her hands, the icy pavement cold through her gloves. With a sigh, she glanced around. She was blessedly alone. She tilted her face skyward and savored the warm sun. Buds were showing on the trees and birds were chattering like mad. Spring was technically here, but it would be another few weeks before the last of the snow as gone. Winter held onto Maine. Once it released its grip, the transition into spring was glorious in its contrast.

She gingerly shifted her weight and straightened her legs. Thorny branches clung to the fabric of her running tights. She tore them free and gathered her energy to stand and run back home on her now bruised leg and hip. The sound of tires on pavement was clear through the quiet morning.

"Fuck," she said to no one. The last thing she wanted was someone to see her in a heap by the side of the road.

She started to clamber up, but she wasn't fast enough. A black SUV came around the bend, slowing immediately and coming to a stop on the opposite side of the road. Of course, it just had to be someone helpful. With a sigh, she brushed her hair out of her face and carefully stood. The windows to the vehicle were tinted, so she couldn't see who it was. She didn't know everyone in Catamount, Maine, but she knew most everyone. The door opened and Shana's pulse rocketed. Hayden Thorne stepped out, a man she certainly didn't expect to see. Her belly clenched, and heat raced through her body.

Hayden slipped a pair of sunglasses off, his caramel eyes meeting hers. A hint of surprise was reflected in his, the only thing giving her a tiny glimmer of relief. He walked across the road, his stride long and powerful. He was tall and lanky with hair that almost exactly matched his eyes.

"Shana, are you okay?"

She nodded jerkily. "Yup. I'm fine, just a little slip on the ice." Her hip throbbed its disagreement, but she ignored it. She'd become the master at ignoring pain over the past winter after her life blew up in her face last year. Physical pain was nothing.

Hayden's eyes coasted over her, assessing. He looked as if he was about to say something else until he met her eyes. Whatever he saw there changed his mind. "Well, how about I give you a ride? Even if you're fine, falling on cold pavement sucks."

Shana's heart thumped—hard. Her hip,

which appeared to have developed its own separate being and mind, nudged her. A ride home would be lovely and far more comforting than trying to run three miles mostly uphill to get back home.

Before she could reply, Hayden continued. "I suppose I could start with hello. Did Dane mention I was coming out here for a visit?"

No, her older brother most certainly had not told her. But then, Dane and most of her friends continued to try to keep her in a bubble when it came to anything that had to do with the mess her late-husband, Callen Peyton, had left behind. Hayden Thorne was a mountain lion shifter from Montana who worked for the Feds. He'd been a big help when she'd bolted out there last year to unravel the secrets Callen left hidden until his death on a highway on Connecticut.

A mountain lion getting hit by a car on the highway in Connecticut was news no matter how you sliced it. Eastern mountain lions had been considered extinct for half a century though rumors swirled that they still lived. Callen's death had burst onto the news, but only Catamount shifters knew the truth. Mountain lions had evolved to become shifters—shifting back and forth from lion to human at will. Catamount, Maine was one of their strongholds in the East. Shana came from a long line of shifters and had married Callen Peyton because it seemed like everyone thought she should. If only she'd listened to her heart, she wouldn't have felt like such a fool when she found out Callen had gotten in deep with a drug smuggling network and started trying to find ways to sell the services of Catamount shifters to the highest bidder. His efforts led to his death after a ridiculous attempt to demonstrate shifters could safely navigate in lion form through the busier parts of the Northeast.

"Shana?"

She swung her gaze up to Hayden, swearing to herself. She'd completely zoned out in front of the one man who seemed capable of thawing the ice around her heart.

"Oh, right. Um, sure. A ride would be good. It's slicker out this morning than I thought."

She figured if she refused the ride, it would make more waves than if she went along with it. Hayden glanced around, his eyes assessing the area. He exuded a quiet, watchful power and strength. Damn if he wasn't knee-weakening sexy. His eyes, like hot caramel, landed on her again.

"Shall we?" he asked, gesturing toward the SUV.

Shana nodded and began to walk across the road. Hobble was the more accurate term. Despite her best efforts, her hip was stiff and tight, throbbing with pain from its collision with the pavement. Hayden stopped and stepped to her side. His hand slipped around her back, his touch burning hot.

"Take it easy," he said, his voice low and warm. "You insist you're fine, but I'm not so sure. Should I take you...?"

She cut him off, waving her hand dismissively. "No, no. I don't need to go anywhere but home. It was a hard fall, but a hot shower is all I need."

Her voice sounded shrill to her. *Great, just great. You sound like a cranky bitch. Well, lately I have been a cranky bitch. How about you cut me some slack?* Her inner critic slouched to the corner. She couldn't quite think about the fact that she hated how she felt lately. Two of her closest friends had found love recently. Happy as she was for them, and she truly was, a tiny corner of her tattered heart wanted to scream and stomp its feet. Maybe she hadn't loved Callen—though no one, not even her closest friends knew that—but she'd tried to make their marriage work for the sake of...

Who was she kidding? For the sake of no one other than Callen, she'd been too embarrassed to admit the marriage had been an utter sham. When he died, she'd been stunned. She had genuinely been sad at first because, even if she didn't love him the way she thought she should have, she had cared for him and never wanted to see any shifter die after getting hit by a car. Such an undignified death, a travesty for a majestic creature. But then, Callen's secrets spilled out for the world to see. Now, she had to face the shame of not knowing what he'd been doing and somehow move on with her life.

She'd thrown herself into helping with the investigation into Callen's drug smuggling and gone to Montana in search of Callen's connections. Months ago, Callen's father had been arrested, along with his brothers and a few other accomplices. For all intents and purposes, Catamount had moved on.

Meanwhile, her heart felt encased in ice. The moment she laid eyes on Hayden in

Montana, the ice cracked. He was like no one she'd ever encountered. Tall and lanky with a deceptive strength, he carried himself almost lazily, but she'd seen him in action. As a mountain lion, he took her breath away. As a human, he sent her heart racing and heat unfurling through her veins. She'd come within a breath of kissing him in Montana. She had told no one about her unannounced visit to his office one afternoon in Montana. Thinking about it now suffused her with liquid heat. She remembered his eyes, burning into her, his lips, inches away. Before he swore and stepped back, his eyes shuttering. He was a man of honor. That she knew. He respected her brother and wouldn't dare take advantage of her. Bitterly, she considered that he probably thought her weak and needy because of what happened.

Her mind returned to the present, Hayden's palm warm on her back, his other hand cupping her elbow. Somehow, she kept it together while he helped her inside. The vehicle was blessedly warm.

Hayden turned to her. "You're gonna have to tell me where to go. Dane gave me directions to his place, but otherwise, I have no idea where I'm going."

"Lucky for you, I live in the guesthouse on Dane's property."

He arched a brow. "Oh? Okay then. We'll just let my GPS tell us where to go then. You can let me know if there's a quicker way."

"What brings you out here? Last I heard, things were mostly resolved with the smuggling network in Catamount."

He nodded as he slowly pulled off the side of the road. "That's what I've heard from Jake and Dane. Problem is, things are still running hot out in Montana. Dane suggested maybe I could get some info from the guys here sitting in jail while they wait for their cases to go to court. The federal prosecutor in Montana is working with the office in Portland to see if they can work out a deal if these guys will help us out on the other side."

"Oh. Well, that makes sense." Hayden almost passed the entrance to Dane's house. "Hey, turn..."

His GPS intoned its instructions right when she started to speak. He caught her eyes and chuckled before slowing and turning abruptly.

Shana took in the familiar landscape as they drove down the winding lane leading to the estate. Dane lived in their childhood home, which was an old colonial farmhouse, stately and lovely. After Callen died, it was all she could do to even walk in the home they had shared. Dane and his new fiancée, Chloe, had offered to let her stay with them in the main house, but Shana needed privacy. She'd moved into an old renovated barn, which had been converted into a modern guesthouse.

She directed Hayden to the guesthouse, which was a good mile away from the main home. He parked the car and leapt out. Before she had a chance to move, he was at the passenger door and opened the door. She started to move, too fast for her stiff hip, and gracelessly fell against him. Hayden's arms caught her easily. Her eyes slammed into his. Time stopped. Her pulse quickened, her breath became shallow. The pull she felt toward him was so strong, she was powerless to resist.

He froze in place, though she could feel his heart pounding where her breast mashed again his rock-hard chest. His eyes darkened and his eyes flicked to her mouth. With thought impossible, she acted on instinct, lifting her free hand and stroking it through his golden brown hair and down along his cheek, savoring the rough stubble. His breath hissed before his lips crashed against hers. The ice inside her melted into liquid heat pulsing through her veins, twisting in her core. His lips feasted on hers, his tongue diving in, sweeping through her mouth. Her tongue tangled with his as she pressed closer, desperate for the heat he offered, the intense feeling he stoked inside of her.

Sensation prickled along her skin, slivers of fire. Wet heat built between her legs, and she shifted restlessly. Finally feeling something after so long was so unbelievably good, she could hardly stand it. It didn't help matters that Hayden kissed like no other. Soft and slow, rough and fast—the combination drugging her senses, taking her breath away, making her want more and more. He abruptly tore his lips away.

She wasn't ready for him to move yet, and he didn't. He hooked an arm on the doorframe, his breath coming in gusts against her cheek. She closed her eyes, savoring his warmth, his strength. Sensation pinged low in her belly, warm and sweet. She almost sobbed in relief. She could feel, and she didn't care that perhaps she should be embarrassed.

"I shouldn't have done that," he said, his voice tight.

She opened her eyes to find his trained on her. His pulse beat visibly in his neck. "I started it," she whispered. "It's okay."

For a second, she thought he might kiss her again, but he slowly straightened. Her eyes flicked down and saw the bulge in his jeans. She resisted the urge to stroke him through the denim. She couldn't help the tiny thrill of knowing she had that effect on him.

"Maybe so, but I know you've been through a lot this year. You don't need me acting like an idiot." He took a step back. His mouth curled up in a wry smile. "You're damn beautiful, so it makes it hard."

She tried to recall the last time any man had called her beautiful. Callen had largely ignored her the last few years, making her self-esteem drain slowly away. She batted the memory away and met Hayden's eyes. She couldn't help her return smile.

SHANA'S slow smile nearly undid him. He had to yank the reins of his control to keep from kissing her again. Fuck. He was in serious trouble. He'd conveniently forgotten how insanely tempting Shana Ashworth was with her glossy honeyed locks that fell in waves halfway down her back, her smoky gray eyes, and her sensual, full mouth. Adding to the temptation, her body was all lush curves and strength.

Hayden had spent his life around mountain lion shifters. Female shifters were renowned for their beauty. Shana took it to another level, primarily due to her natural sultry manner and complete obliviousness to how delectable she was. He recalled meeting her in Montana and being relieved he'd been seated at a table. He respected her brother and knew she'd been through a lot, so it absolutely wasn't okay for him to be battling a hard on every time he came near her.

AVAILABLE NOW!
Destined Mate

GO HERE to sign up for information on new releases: http://jhcroixauthor.com/subscribe/

FIND MY BOOKS

Thank you for reading Fated Mate! I hope you enjoyed the story. If so, you can help other readers find my books in a variety of ways.

1) Write a review!
2) Sign up for my newsletter, so you can receive information about upcoming new releases & receive a FREE copy of one of my books: http://jhcroixauthor.com/subscribe/
3) Like and follow my Amazon Author page at https://amazon.com/author/jhcroix
4) Follow me on Bookbub at https://www.bookbub.com/authors/j-h-croix
5) Follow me on Instagram at https://www.instagram.com/jhcroix/

6) Like my Facebook page at https://www.
facebook.com/jhcroix

CATAMOUNT LION SHIFTERS
Protected Mate
Chosen Mate
Fated Mate
Destined Mate
A Catamount Christmas
The Lion Within
Lion Lost & Found
Swoon Series
This Crazy Love
Wait For Me
Break My Fall
Truly Madly Mine
Into The Fire Series
Burn For Me
Slow Burn
Burn So Bad
Hot Mess
Burn So Good
Sweet Fire
Play With Fire
Melt With You
Burn For You

Crash & Burn

Brit Boys Sports Romance

The Play

Big Win

Out Of Bounds

Play Me

Naughty Wish

Diamond Creek Alaska Novels

When Love Comes

Follow Love

Love Unbroken

Love Untamed

Tumble Into Love

Christmas Nights

Last Frontier Lodge Novels

Christmas on the Last Frontier

Love at Last

Just This Once

Falling Fast

Stay With Me

When We Fall

Hold Me Close

Crazy For You

Just Us

ACKNOWLEDGMENTS

Yet again, I close the last chapter of each book with huge thanks to my husband for his support and for still making me laugh every day. My editor, Laura Kingsley, holds me to a high standard and helps me make each book as good as it can be. Clarise Tan at CT Cover Creations not only designs stunning covers, but she's a joy to work with. Always...my readers: thank you from the bottom of my heart for supporting my books with such enthusiasm.

xoxo
J.H. Croix

ABOUT THE AUTHOR

USA Today Bestselling Author J. H. Croix lives in a small town in the historical farmlands of Maine with her husband and two spoiled dogs. Croix writes contemporary romance with sassy women and alpha men who aren't afraid to show some emotion. Her love for quirky small-towns and the characters that inhabit them shines through in her writing. Take a walk on the wild side of romance with her bestselling novels!

Places you can find me:
jhcroixauthor.com
jhcroix@jhcroix.com